FOLD AND DIE

FOLD AND DIE

A Jordan Lacey Mystery

Stella Whitelaw

This first world edition published 2009
in Great Britain and in the USA by
SEVERN HOUSE PUBLISHERS LTD of
9–15 High Street, Sutton, Surrey, England, SM1 1DF.
Trade paperback edition published
in Great Britain and the USA 2010 by
SEVERN HOUSE PUBLISHERS LTD

British Library Cataloguing in Publication Data

Whitelaw, Stella.
  Fold and Die.
  1. Lacey, Jordan (Fictitious character) – Fiction. 2. Women
  private investigators – Fiction. 3. Cruise ships – Fiction.
  4. Murder – Investigation – Fiction. 5. Detective and mystery stories.
  I. Title
  823.9'14-dc22

ISBN-13: 978-0-7278-6806-0   (cased)
ISBN-13: 978-1-84751-172-0   (trade paper)

*To Agnes Hareide, husband Roger and daughter Sara
who took me on a wonderful day in Alesund*

Typeset by Palimpsest Book Production Ltd.,
Grangemouth, Stirlingshire, Scotland.
Printed and bound in Great Britain by
MPG Books Ltd., Bodmin, Cornwall.

ONE

'You've got to come with me. Someone is trying to kill me. If you don't come with me, I'll be dead by next week.'

The woman was hysterical, her face contorted with fear. She was an attractive-looking woman with well-cut light blonde hair that would cost a weekly fortune at the hairdressers. Her eyes were blue, eyebrows finely plucked, mouth framed in glossy strawberry lipstick. But no pretty smile now. Her lips were puckered with distress.

'I'm really sorry, Mrs Carter, but I'm far too busy to get away.' It was a total lie. I hadn't had a new case for weeks but there was something about Joanna Carter that gave me the creeps. I don't accept work from people who give me the creeps.

We were talking in the café on Latching pier, the sea lapping its legs. Joanna Carter wanted to meet in a public place. She wouldn't come to the office behind my shop. She said she wouldn't feel safe. What could be safer than a shop full of first class odds and ends, shelves of books and harmless junk?

My detective agency was called First Class Investigations and my shop First Class Junk, both were brilliant titles. I had a job living up to them. My reputation for self-induced catastrophes was well known around Latching. Latching was a West Sussex coastal town, four miles of beach and churning sea, a delightful, eccentric resort, with beautiful Georgian and Regency buildings side by side with disastrous multi-storey car parks and other hideous Sixties monstrosities. Shoot the planners who pulled down the old houses. Fortunately most of them were already dead. Maybe they'd turn in their graves, shift the turf.

'But, Miss Lacey, I'm willing to pay for your protection. You must come as my bodyguard. I shall die if you don't come with me.'

'I really don't see what I could do.'

'You'd be there, at my side, every minute of the day
and night. You'd be my visible protection. No one would
dare to kill me if they saw that I was never entirely alone.'

My heart sank. That never alone bit was ominous. It was
awkward enough being in the company of Mrs Carter for
the time it took to swallow a cup of coffee. And the heat
was scalding my mouth.

'I'm not a trained bodyguard,' I said. 'I'm a private
investigator.'

'I know,' she said, her face momentarily lightening.
'That's what's so perfect. You don't look like a detective.
You look unusual and eccentric. They would never suspect
you. They'd think you were some friend tagging along.'

'I'm great at tagging along,' I said. 'And what if they
found out that I was a private detective and they bump me
off first?'

'But then, at least I'd have a chance of getting away.
Don't you see?'

Nice one. I liked her even less.

Mrs Carter's story was a fairly normal one. She had been
separated from her husband, Oliver, for some years, it
seemed. No reason given. She clammed up each time I tried
to extract a little more information out of her. Incompatibility
or something, she said. He liked Marmite and she didn't?
Or some difference of opinion that was equally inane? They
had no children.

However, now she was convinced that he had hired an
assassin to finish her off. There had been unexplained
accidents and incidents. Someone had put a burning rag
through her letterbox. It might have been the newspaper
boy who was sick of her complaints? She had been nearly
run over by a speeding car. Maybe she stepped out into the
road without looking? She had received something horrid
in the post but she wouldn't say what.

'It was enough to have frightened the life out of me,'
she added, shuddering. Probably dead road-kill. 'And
there have been phone calls. The empty kind with nobody
there.'

It happens to all of us. Some financial company in China or India, cold calling all the numbers in the book.

She had rung me almost immediately after the something nasty in the post. That's how we came to be meeting in the café on the pier. I made sure that I got the window seat with a sea view. I'm partial to sea view healing. I daily walked the pier, eight minutes round trip, my tawny hair streaming, face lifted to whatever wind force was being thrown at me. Force nine hurls me back, has me grabbing the railings.

'But why do you think someone is out to kill you?'

'I know, I just feel it. Sometimes I know there is someone in the garden or prowling round outside the house. That's why I've decided to go away for two weeks on a cruise. I need a break from being watched all the time.'

'Why don't you talk to the police about your fears, get them to post someone outside your house?'

'I don't want the police involved,' she gulped, her voice rising, hands trembling. 'They would definitely kill me if they thought I had been to the police. I mean, no one wants to get involved with the police, do they?'

'Thank you very much for the coffee, Mrs Carter,' I said. I'd had enough of these hysterics. 'But I really do have to decline your offer. Perhaps you should go to the police and report your suspicions. Now, I have to go back to my office, I've a pile of paperwork to get done.'

'Fifty thousand pounds,' she said.

It was quite difficult to restart the leaving process after that announcement. I metaphorically picked myself off the floor of the pier café, my legs refusing to obey explicit moving instructions. That morning I'd had a letter from both my landlords saying that the rent on my shop and my flat was going up yet again. The current spiralling inflation and credit crunch wasn't helping my financial situation. The odds on my refusing this job were suddenly dramatically reduced.

'I'll think about it,' I said. I'd think about it for about three minutes and then find myself some more salubrious work. Like stacking shelves.

'Well, don't take too long about it, Miss Lacey. The ship sails at four p.m. the day after tomorrow. And I'm going, whatever you decide. If it's yes, then you'd better be at Southampton docks by two p.m. And bring some decent clothes. They have a very strict dress code.'

'Dress code?' Whatever was the woman talking about? MI5?

'Yes, four formal, six semi-casual and four casual.'

I went cold even though the weather was a balmy fifteen Celsius in Latching, West Sussex. I didn't have a dress code. My code was jeans and shirt, jeans and sweater, jeans and vest top. Call me an impulsive dresser. I only own two dresses. A second-hand frothy blue one that was given to me to wear to a party, and a plain black from my shop assistant surveillance job. My box of gear at the shop was great for disguises but I doubted if the cruise company would class a bag lady as formal.

'Formal is very smart,' she said. 'For the captain's cock-tail party and various other events that need dressing up.'

'Dressing up,' I repeated again. Surely dressing up was for six-year-olds in their mother's high heels?

'I'll leave you to sort out your wardrobe but I'll see you at the Queen Elizabeth Terminal at Southampton docks at two o'clock. Be on time. I've hired a car but I'm sure there is a good train service from Latching.'

'I haven't said that I'm coming,' I said, dredging up some degree of independence, determined not to be dragooned into this job. I've done a lot of funny cases, finding lost tortoises, stolen puppies, disappearing husbands, and a night-watch up a tree to trap a garden desecrator. 'I have several other commitments.'

'It's only two weeks,' she said. Joanna Carter suddenly looked vulnerable. 'And this is life and death. My life, my death. You do have a passport, don't you?'

Fortunately my years in the police force had provided me with an up-to-date passport. It was my let-out clause. I could say no. I could pretend that I didn't have one of those maroon covered booklets with a photo of a bug-eyed female Dracula.

'Yes, I do.'

'That's all settled, then,' said Joanna Carter, gathering up her Gucci bag and stylish trench coat. The weather in Latching was up the creek. The seasons had gone haywire. It was early June and no one had shed a layer yet. Where was summer hiding? Was it behind one of the newly painted beach huts?

She was gone before I could repeat my lack of interest in her proposition. Fifty thousand pounds was a ridiculous amount of money to pay for two weeks' work. I had never earned so much, even when I had solved a case and occasionally received a surprise reward for a lost this or that.

I sat in Maeve's Café with another coffee. I needed the caffeine to calm my nerves. Latching was a seaside town in West Sussex nestled in a valley with the rolling South Downs curving a benevolent arm round the outskirts. I loved every inch of it, especially the sea. A cruise would be acres of bonus sea, huge waves and sparkling wake. How would I cope with so much sea?

And how I loved the sea. Not every inch of it as that's the wrong measurement for liquid. But every wave, every trough, every drop, every speck of foaming white horse. I loved its changing moods, could stand for hours, buffeted by the wind, watching the great coffee-coloured waves rolling diagonally on to the beach, churning the sand, washing the pebbles, lashing the legs of the pier and the groynes. The sea mesmerized me. I was its slave.

I had this corner shop, First Class Junk, which sold practically anything. My stock was bought from charity shops or house auctions. It was a front for First Class Investigations, my detective agency. FCI rhymed with FBI which seemed to give it resonance.

Some distance away I had two bedsits, side by side, but I knew they were going to have to go. The landlords were talking about renovating them into posh holiday flats and charging higher rents. They did no repairs. But they had been perfect for me in the early days. Two rooms, two keys, two kitchen units, two bells that didn't work. No one knew where I was. Very convenient. It would soon be time for me to move on. Perhaps two weeks at sea would give me time to rethink my life.

And there was DI James. The man who was the love of my life. He had been posted to Yorkshire eventually, to the city of York in fact. That historic town with walls you could walk on and a river that regularly flooded. He emailed occasionally but it was not the same. My skin was slowly unfolding for lack of him.

So there I was, lots of things going wrong in my life, empty and purposeless. I was half minded to up and move to York but the sea held me back. And my shop and my agency and my friends. I had a lot of good friends.

'So why the long face?' Doris asked as I went into her nearby grocer's shop for some Soya milk and a couple of apples. I was not a big spender.

'I've been offered a job as a bodyguard,' I said.

'So what weapons are involved?' she asked, practical as ever. 'Guns, knives, garrottes, poison, a hefty push?'

'That's the trouble, she doesn't know. This woman is being threatened and thinks she would be safer with me around. It's not a clear-cut scenario.'

'So it might be a piece of cake,' said Doris, adding a couple of yogurts without being asked. 'It could all be in her imagination. Lots of women get funny ideas. Think they are being stalked. Is she menopausal?'

'I don't know,' I said, pushing some money across the counter. 'She's not an easy woman to get along with. It could be two weeks of purgatory.'

'Go for it, Jordan. Two weeks is nothing. Fourteen days, over in a blink of an eyelid. Where does she live?'

'It's not where she lives, it's where she's going.'

'Where's she going?'

'She's going on a cruise to Norway, to the Arctic, to the North Cape to see the midnight sun.'

Doris stared at me as if I was mad. 'The midnight sun? Jordan, don't be daft. It's the chance of a lifetime. If you don't go, I'll shut shop and go in your place. I'd guard a horde of maniacal criminals for a chance like that. You can't say no to an offer to go to the North Cape.'

'I can say no and I probably will. I've got a very strange feeling about her and I don't like it.'

'How much is she going to pay you?'

'Fifty thousand.'

Even saying it out loud was a shock. I swallowed hard.

Doris fell against the counter and broke one of her long Russian Red nails. Her nails were her pride and joy. They were never chipped or broken. But for once the news had stunned her and she didn't notice the damage.

'You are taking this job, Jordan Lacey, if I have to drag you to the ship by your long red hair. That's an order. Now, what have you got for clothes?'

'Nothing suitable. One blue chiffon dress. Worn twice. She says there's a dress code. What's a dress code?'

'I'm taking you in hand. Shopping.'

'I haven't any money.'

'Did I say couture? We're going charity shopping.'

Now I often go charity shopping but it is for goods for my shop: antiques, books, odds and ends that might dress the two small optician-sized windows. But Doris was into top gear clothes shopping. She presumed that I had enough decent undies and personal garments. My undies are perfect. I have an excessive washing disorder.

'Take your own nighties or pyjamas,' she said. I was a T-shirt sleeper. They would have to do. 'And your good anorak. It'll be cold in the Arctic. You've got thermals, haven't you?'

'Two vests.'

'Take both of them. You'll need two.'

It was going to be cold in the Arctic so winter woollies were necessary as well as all these formal and semi-formal outfits. It was quite fun once you got the hang of it. Straight to the rails of black dresses in the shop for the formal. There were lots of bargains in fleece and warmer clothing. Everyone thought summer might be round the corner and were throwing out layers.

'I didn't say I was going,' I said, as we struggled back to my bedsits with carrier bags of all sizes. Yet I had

spent less than forty-five pounds. I had the four formal
and semi-formal was a variety of striking tops to go with
my best black trousers. One of the formals was a vintage
dream.

'You'll look lovely,' said Doris, as we climbed the stairs
to the first floor. 'People throw out really smashing stuff.
They say that eighty per cent of clothes are never worn.
That long black ruffled evening dress is stunning. Pity, it
doesn't fit me. I'd have it like a shot.'

'You can have it,' I said. 'Let out the seams.'

I'd picked up my post at the front door, shuffling through
it as I put a kettle on for some tea. Doris deserved a rest.
She looked knackered. I'd often thought she was a lot older
than she made out and running a small grocer's shop single-
handed was not easy.

There was a card from DI James. It was a picture of York
Minster, the majestic cathedral that dominated the city.

'Very busy,' he wrote. 'Crime never stops. Going on a
course next week, very hush-hush. Take care, don't do
anything I wouldn't do. James.'

He had signed it with his Christian name. His parents,
in a fit of post-birth dementia, had christened him James.
He was James James. It took some living down. I didn't
blame him.

I opened another envelope with one hand as I made tea
with the other. It's a skill I had acquired. It was a letter
from my landlords, computer printed, Courier New type
face, font 12.

> Dear Miss Lacey,
>   We regret to inform you that we are giving you one
> month's notice to leave your two bedsits. We have
> been given the required council permission to turn the
> building into residential flats.
>   Yours sincerely, etc.

My hand shook as I poured the tea. The teapot was a sweet,
old-fashioned flowered shape that held only two cupfuls.
It had once belonged to a grand family, probably served

the lady of the house with her breakfast-in-bed morning cuppa.

'I've been given notice,' I said. 'One month.'

'Then you have got to go on this cruise,' said Doris, adding a sweetener to her tea. She was always on a diet. 'You'll need that fifty thousand for a deposit.'

'Deposit?'

'You'll have to buy your own place now. No more bedsits, my girl. You need a real home. A proper kitchen and a proper bathroom.'

I suddenly thought about having a real home, a bathroom and a cat. Not about a place of my own, but of having a cat around. I'd always wanted a cat, had several surrogate feline friends, but never had one of my own. Mavis had a cat who liked me, hung around. Perhaps I could endure the coming two cruising weeks for the sake of owning a cat. It was almost worth it.

'But supposing Mrs Carter does get killed?'

'Make her pay you in advance. Fair's fair.'

'But if she is killed, then I haven't done my job properly, so I wouldn't have earned it.'

'Jordan Lacey,' said Doris, with emphasis on each syllable. 'You have more morals than a saint. And saints always come to a sticky end.'

I phoned Joanna Carter before I could change my mind. It was touch and almost no-go. I nearly put the receiver down especially when she asked me to go round to her house that very moment.

'There's someone in the garden,' she said. She really did sound scared. 'You've got to come. Please. I need you. I can hear them moving about.'

'All right,' I said, trying to disguise my indifference. She gave me her address and how to find it. But I knew where her house was immediately. It was The Beeches, Lansfold Avenue, the beautiful double-fronted Edwardian house which had featured in my first ever case.

It was the home of the late Ellen Frances Swantry, the nun. The house had been turned into four spacious flats

and Joanna Carter must have the ground floor flat. One day
I might tell Mrs Carter what the police had found in the
disused air raid shelter in the garden. Or maybe not. It had
been demolished and levelled over.

I took short cuts through various twittens. They were the
narrow alleyways between rows of houses, the escape routes
of smugglers in past times when Latching was the centre of
the smuggling industry. The Beeches had certainly seen
some changes. The stonework had been repainted white,
double glazing in the big bay windows, the heavy front
door varnished and brass knocker polished.

The first development had been a rest home for retired
people but they went broke and the next lot of developers
turned it into four flats, two in the main house, and two in
the new extension built on in the garden.

Memories came flooding back. I had bought Ellen
Swantry's Victorian button-back chair, her Persian rug and
her filing cabinet from a second-hand dealer. They were all
still in good use in my office. They gave it style.

The beech tree in the garden had been pruned and there
was now a manicured lawn and regimental flower beds.
So different from the first time I had seen the house, empty
and neglected. On that first visit I had climbed into the
larder, after loosening a faulty catch on a window. This
time I knocked using the lion's head knocker. Quite an
improvement. I heard bolts being drawn back and a chain
unfastened.

Joanna Carter opened the door a crack. 'Come in, come
in. Be quick,' she hissed. 'Hurry, hurry, please. There's
someone out in the back garden, creeping about. I can hear
them.'

She almost pulled me into the house. At first I was dis-
orientated. The hallway had been divided and a double-size
glass door portioned off the stairs that led to the upper flat.
She ushered me into the front room and I immediately
recognized the shape of the bay windows and the ornate
ceiling cornice. The ugly cast-iron fireplace had been
removed and replaced with a marble Italian copy.

I only had time to glance at the thick white carpet on the

floor and two three-seater sofas facing each other across a long, pale-wood coffee table. She was dragging me towards the back of the flat.

I guessed that the small back sitting room where Ellen had spent most of her days knitting and reading magazines had been turned into a bathroom. It made sense.

The grimy green kitchen and larder, with enamelled gas stove and brown earthenware sink, had long been banished to the municipal dump. This was the latest in kitchen designer ware, more pale-wood panels and cupboards, marble surfaces and eye-level oven and microwave. On the pristine mottled surface was a ceramic tray with two cut-glass tumblers and a decanter of whisky. Or it might have been brandy. I was only an expert on red wine. Had Mrs Carter been entertaining?

She switched off the light and we stood in the dimness. Moonlight filtered through the window with long silver fingers. The window was fitted with blinds and she had not closed them.

'Listen,' she said, pulling me forward. 'What can you hear?'

Silence is funny stuff. The more you shut out everyday noises, the more you realize that the atmosphere is breathing space. There was a sort of low hum from a hot water system, rustling of leaves from nearby beech trees, maybe the howl of a distant fox cub calling for its mother.

'I can't hear anything,' I began. But I stopped. I had heard something. Not sure what it was. Then I heard it again. It was a footstep, quite definitely a footstep on the patio outside.

Half a shiver ran down my spine. There was someone out there. A stray cat doesn't wear shoes. I was not going to investigate. Mrs Carter hadn't paid me a penny yet, so I was not exactly employed by her. I was here more or less as an observer and I could observe safely from behind the kitchen door.

'Do you believe me now?' she whispered.

'Yes.' I nodded. I found myself whispering back. 'There's certainly someone out there. Could it be the tenant of the upstairs flat? Putting out the rubbish or doing a spot of late-night gardening?'

'No, an elderly couple live upstairs, the McDonalds. They're away visiting their grandchildren in Dorset. It's not either of them.'

'What about the tenants in the annexe?'

'Both retired ladies. They don't go out after dark.'

There was an array of bolts and chains on the back door, all securely fastened, brass glistening.

'Let's leave whoever it is to their nocturnal wanderings,' I said, moving Mrs Carter back to her elegant white sitting room. She had drawn the ivory velvet curtains. It was a very white room. The only colour was from the velvet scatter cushions and even they were the palest lemon and gold.

'Beautiful room,' I murmured, sitting down without being asked. The sofa enveloped me in softness. I pushed a cushion into the small of my back for support.

'It was designed by Estelle Warburton,' said Joanna Carter. 'You may have heard of her. She's a very up and coming interior decorator.'

No, I hadn't heard of her and she certainly wasn't going to design anything for me. I liked some colour around me. Then I thought of the black evening dress I had bought today and wondered if there was some contradiction there.

'You may recall that we were discussing payment for two weeks of personal bodyguarding,' I said. Not exactly true, as we had not reached the financing of the work. I thought adding the word *personal* was a nice touch.

'Yes,' she said, suddenly brisk, her composure recovered. 'I shall pay you half at the start and half at the end. That way I'll be sure that you do your job properly and effi-ciently. I don't want you propping up a bar all evening with the ship's officers instead of looking after me.'

'I don't prop up bars,' I said icily, suddenly not liking her again. 'And since I should like to deposit the money in my bank before we leave, I shall expect you to write me a cheque this evening, now, before I go.'

Joanna Carter looked surprised at this show of no nonsense from someone with a reputation of undercharging or even completely forgetting to charge a client who couldn't afford me.

'Yes, of course,' she said, going to a French lacquered writing desk in the corner of the room. 'Twenty thousand?'

'Half of fifty is twenty-five.'

'How silly of me. I'm still feeling a little upset.' She drew up a chair and wrote out a cheque. Even the pen seemed reluctant and she had to shake it several times. 'There you are, Miss Lacey. All signed and sealed.'

'And I have a client form for you to fill in. It is a simple form. Just a few details. Nothing too complicated, but I need to have some information. Mobile phone number, email, etc. And I'll give you my card.'

'Of course, Miss Lacey. I'll do it now.'

'And I think you could call me Jordan, if we are to be travelling companions. Perhaps we should cook up some story to cover the situation. I could be a long-lost cousin from New Zealand, or the daughter of a school friend, recovering from a life-threatening illness. Sea air and all that.'

She looked a little faint. 'Yes, I suppose we'll have to have some sort of cover story about why we are travelling together and who you are. People do ask a lot of questions on cruises. It's an occupational hazard.'

I pocketed the cheque and heaved myself out of the softness. The sight of all those noughts had cheered me up immensely. 'That'll be my first job,' I said. 'I'll think up something really watertight and plausible. Goodnight, Mrs Carter. Lock up behind me.'

'Do you really have to go?'

'Yes, I do. You'll be all right now. Whoever it was has gone, I'm sure. And I have to get home. You've only given me a day to pack.'

'If you are sure he's gone . . .'

'Quite sure. Not a sound.'

She opened the front door cautiously. The neat path was luminous and looked safe enough. I was not being threatened. I would be safe. My client was the target, not me. Suddenly I realized how difficult this job was going to be.

I should have to give it some thought. Perhaps DI James could help me. I'd email him tomorrow in York.

Suddenly Mrs Carter grabbed my arm and pointed to the beech tree. She was trembling, her mouth hung open. I looked towards the tree. A low bough was swaying in the breeze. There was something hanging from the branch. Something pale and long with a looped and knotted end.

It was a hangman's noose.

TWO

Southampton

I was treacle-eyed with train lag. Latching to Southampton Central was a straightforward train journey, vaguely downhill, but with so many station stops, I began to wonder if I was taking the scenic route via the Lake District. Nor was I used to taking care of luggage. The expanding beige on brown Louis Vuitton suitcase which Mavis had lent me had a foreign look, nothing to do with me, guv.

It obviously impressed the taxi driver who drove me on to the cruise terminal from Southampton Central. If I could afford a case like that, and was a passenger on a cruise ship, then I could afford a few pounds extra on the fare.

'And don't think of overcharging me,' I said, as he drew up outside the vast departures hall. It looked like a corrugated aircraft hangar. Somewhere behind it loomed a huge white ship shape with portholes. It seemed to go on forever, like a block of flats. It didn't resemble a ship, not the kind of ship shape I was used to. 'Your tax disc is out of date.'

I said it in my best ex-WPO voice and it threw his attention. His wheels bumped the kerb stone.

'Sorry, miss,' he said. 'The meter's not working properly.'

'It's not working at all.'

Joanna Carter's cheque was safely in the bank so I could afford a decent tip. She had said nothing about expenses, but I preferred to pay for some things myself. It would give me an element of independence. She might think she owned me, body and soul, but I had other plans for the separate parts of my body.

The formalities of checking in were easy. Joanna had travelled overnight to Southampton, refusing to stay in The Beeches another minute after the noose in the tree incident.

It was pretty scary, I'll admit. She was already packed and ordered a taxi. I stayed with her till it arrived.

'If I've forgotten anything, I can b–buy it on–b–board,' she said, downing another brandy in one. I removed the noose from the tree so she didn't have to look at it again. I put it in a plastic bag, forensic training, just in case, and it was lodged in a safe place. Back room of my office.

Cruise card in hand I climbed up the steep gangway on to the ship, the aluminium steps clattering. The MV *Orpheus Odyssey* soared above me, a great sweep of white wall, dotted with cabins and portholes and red lifeboats. The decks towered like a huge building, only the red funnel and the shape of her bows giving away that it was a ship. I was stunned by the size and the stillness despite the noise and bustle on the quay. I couldn't see any water. But I could hear it, lapping away somewhere.

At the top of the gangway, security checked the cruise card, now called a swipe card, through a scanning machine. It was all very high tech.

'Do you know where my case is, please?' I asked the uniformed steward who came forward in reception. He looked as if he was about to whisk me away to some far-off place. I would never see land again.

'It will be safely delivered to your cabin, madam. It will be there very soon. You have your cabin number? I will show you the way.'

It was among all the bits of paper I had been given. Mrs Carter had booked adjoining staterooms on A Deck, inter-connecting doors. This meant nothing to me. At least I wouldn't have to sleep in the same cabin, endure endless frantic chat.

'No, thank you,' I said hurriedly. I wanted a few last minutes to myself. 'I think I'll go on deck. Last glimpse of England and all that.'

'Yes, madam. Promenade deck or lido deck. The lift will take you.'

I escaped his attentions. I half expected him to escort me to the lift and press the button. Any top button would do. It couldn't go any further than the top deck. Unless there was a lift going to the funnel.

The docks were a forest of cranes and ships, cruise and cargo, clustered round an industrial area. It stretched for miles, coping with a double tide. Southampton had tower blocks of housing and offices, like any other thriving city, but somewhere there were the crumbling stone walls of an ancient city threading their solid way through today's commercial areas. What would those merchants of long ago have thought of this bustling place with its one-way streets and endless blinking traffic lights?

For the first time today I relaxed against the rails and absorbed the drama of the docks and the lapping water. The sea looked so far down below and fathomlessly dark. I had never seen it from this viewpoint and it gave me a tremor of vertigo. The highest viewpoint I ever got in Latching was from the pier.

If I could still see the sea, I might enjoy this cruise after all. The sea was my life, my hope, my joy. Maybe I could lock Joanna Carter into her cabin for the duration, sorry, stateroom.

Something about the ship, *Orpheus Odyssey*, grabbed me at that moment. She was big, so majestic, yet she was tethered to the dock like a prisoner, unable to move. Those heavy tethering ropes held her prisoner. How could I feel empathy with something so gigantic? But I did. She was a sea-sailing, floating colossus, enormously powerful, ready to battle oceans and winds and tides, yet at this moment, she was floating by the quay, helpless.

I felt a shiver. A sweet-faced Thai girl appeared at my side. She was holding a tray of drinks. 'Champagne? Sail away party?' she asked.

'Lovely,' I said.

The flutes were champagne shaped so that must indicate the sparkling contents. A brass band was playing some-where. This must be what they called a sail away party. I couldn't see any party happening.

'Thank you,' I said, thinking they were free.

'Cruise card, please.' She produced a bill pad and a pen.

New procedure for me. I duly signed, remembering to be warned in future. Nothing was free. This was how they made their money. Cabin prices might be reasonable for the distance and the lavish life style, but once on board some cruise ships wanted you to spend, spend, spend.

The band on the dockside was playing a stirring Sousa march. John Philip, American composer and band leader of marches, still being played all over the world. Then they turned to the heart-wrenching *'We are sailing, we are sailing . . .'* and I suddenly realized that things were happening. It was too late to jump off.

It was a few minutes after five o'clock. Those huge ropes were being thrown off the quayside and a tug called *Bentley* was pulling the ship out into the water. It seemed a tricky manoeuvre because I could feel there was a strong current astern. We were heading towards the Fawley Oil Terminal. I had never seen it from this aspect or distance before. We were travelling along the Southampton water in a stately manner. The Southampton Patrol were making sure the small, curious pleasure craft kept out of our way.

All this part of the coast was achingly familiar to me. After leaving Calshot Spit, we went along the narrow Thorn Channel before turning around Brambles Bank, and setting course along the Solent. I thrived on the feeling of being on a big ship, powerful and dominant, ploughing through the sea. Sea everywhere but still land in sight. Or perhaps it was the bubbly sail-away champagne giving me a false sense of security.

I recognized the forts off Portsmouth. A lot further along the coast, but out of sight, was Latching. My home town. But I wouldn't be seeing it for two weeks. I got a lurch of homesickness and gripped the rail tighter.

I didn't know where we were. I didn't even know exactly where we were going. One thing was sure. *Orpheus Odyssey* and I were already in sync. We were a team. This big ship and I.

'So you've found your way up on deck.' It was Joanna Carter. She looked more relaxed than the last time I saw her. She was wearing a tailored white trouser suit, gilt trimmed buttons and belt. I felt quite scruffy beside her despite clean black jeans, new white T-shirt and my faithful black leather jacket. 'Impressive, isn't it?'

'Very.'

'Our last view of England.'

'Goodbye, England.'

'Your luggage has arrived. We've adjoining staterooms on A Deck with an interconnecting door. It's normally used for families but it suits us perfectly. I shall expect the door to be kept open at all times.'

'Great.' I was going into incommunicative mood again. What was it about this woman that built the Berlin Wall single-handed?

'It's only two decks down from here. We ought to hurry. I think we should dress for dinner, although it is informal tonight. We're first sitting. Let's go.'

'First sitting?'

'There are two sittings, first and second, in the Delphi dining room. First sitting is at six thirty and the second at eight thirty. It has to serve two lots of diners and we are first sitting.'

'It's too early. I'm not hungry,' I said. Six thirty felt like barely tea time, scones and sponge cake round the nursery fire.

'You've no choice,' she said.

I wanted to stay on deck. I wanted to watch the coast line slipping away. The Isle of Wight was familiar to me. It was about walking tours along the coast and Carisbrooke Castle and Osborne House. I'd once been climbing up Alum Bay cliffs and got stuck halfway. A seventeen-year-old boy rescued me. My first crush. His name was Michael Thorogood. Nothing came of it. My usual luck.

I followed my employer down two flights of plush stairs to A Deck. There were paintings along all the walls. They became my signposts. Three yachts, one red-sailed, and I was heading in the right direction whether we were going stern or aft. Down a long corridor to A708 and A710 and we were there. They were the last two staterooms along that corridor. The door at the end of the corridor opened out on to a deck area, quoits and shuffleboard. I could see

sunlight through the window and vaguely a froth of sea.
Mentally I marked it as an escape route. 'Your stateroom
is A710,' said Mrs Carter. 'I'm next door but the communicating door must be kept open at all times. I still don't
feel safe.'

'Naturally.' I was running out of things to say to her.

I went into my cabin, or stateroom as Joanna kept
calling it. Was I expecting bunk beds? For a moment I
was stunned. It was luxurious. For years I had been living
in two cramped bedsits. Easy to live in, keep clean, tidy.
But the stateroom was amazing. I wander round, like it
was a dream. Pinch me.

In the brochure it was called an outside stateroom with
balcony. King-sized bed. Full-sized bath and shower. Lounge
area with sofa, coffee table and chair. I hoped I'd have some
free time to sit on the sofa. TV and radio, writing desk,
refrigerator, etc. But most of all, floor to ceiling patio doors
leading to balcony with table and chairs. It was fantastic.
Don't ask me about decor, sort of pale wood everywhere.
I went instantly colour-blind.

'Do you like it?' Joanna hovered in the doorway, wrapped
in a voluminous bath towel. She'd been taking a shower
already. That woman could move.

'It's wonderful,' I said, still opening cupboards and
drawers like a demented housekeeper. My cruise clothes
would fit into a quarter of the space.

'Dinner will be served in twenty minutes,' she said,
humming to herself.

I was beginning to think this case would be wasting my
time. What ever could happen on this floating paradise to
harm Mrs Carter? She would be cocooned and watched
over every minute of the day by stewards, waiters, crew,
officers, all taking personal care of her. Every passenger
was screened and scrutinized before coming aboard. No
knives, bombs or guns in luggage. She was safe. Safe as
houses or ships, whatever.

My luggage had been delivered to my cabin. I hung up
clothes and stowed undies and jerseys into drawers, but half
of the wardrobe was still empty. I put my few cosmetics in

the bathroom cabinet. The eye shadow and mascara looked lonely on the shelf beside the complimentary toiletries. There were big white towels stacked in the bathroom, enough to last me a week. And a brand new white face flannel folded on the shelf. That impressed me. A new fluffy face flannel. It felt so soft. Lots of fabric conditioner?

'You missed the muster call,' said Joanna. 'Where were you?'

'I was on deck,' I said. 'Watching us sail away.'

'You are supposed to go to it, to learn how to put on your life jacket.'

'I guess I could work it out in an emergency. A few Velcro straps.'

'You have to go to your muster station. Ours is in the Olympus theatre.'

'But supposing that's the end that's sinking? Then where do we go?'

She shot me a hard look and sniffed. 'I've no idea.'

I was tired of this conversation. How could I survive twenty-four hours a day non-stop chatter and recriminations? The noose on the branch had been a hoax. A neighbour maddened to distraction. This was all a farce. I was being taken for a ride. The cheque had probably bounced. She wanted a companion, slave, a servant, someone to boss around.

'Come on, you'd better hurry and get changed. I said that we're the first sitting tonight.'

I was wearing something simple. I dug my heels in. I might wash my face and hands (like Eliza Doolittle) but I was not changing my clothes. They were all clean on this morning.

A flash of annoyance crossed Joanna's face as I re-appeared later, still in my black jeans and white T-shirt. She pulled a waistcoat from her wardrobe. It was red and white striped brocade. It stirred a memory. I'd seen it before. Had I worn it somewhere before?

'Put this on,' she said. 'We can't have you looking like a starving student.'

I put on the waistcoat but said nothing. Words would

have choked me. Now she was dressing me and I was wearing her clothes. How much worse could it get?

I followed her out of the cabin, sorry stateroom, along the corridor to the lifts. I had no idea where I was going. There were a lot of well-dressed people stiffly waiting for the lift.

'I could walk,' I offered, seeing a continuation of the stairs.

'You're staying with me,' she said, between her teeth, as she smiled at complete strangers. Everyone was feeling new and strange, kept a distance and stiff British reserve, nodding and smiling. 'Don't you dare ever leave me.'

The Delphi dining room was down on the reception deck. I recognized the central statue of Orpheus, the most famous poet and musician who ever lived. He was holding a lyre, about to pluck a string and never quite making it.

'Legend says that trees and rocks followed his music,' I said as we went into the dining room, welcomed by smiling waiters and staff. We were shown to a table. I'd never seen a room so opulent, such sparkling chandeliers. There was gleaming silver and glass on the tables and pristine white cloths and folded napkins.

'What nonsense,' said Joanna. 'Wherever did you get that rubbish? A table for six, number seventeen, that's ours, very nice. We shall have some company and people to talk to. We're first to arrive so we have first choice where to sit. You sit there and watch the door. I don't want my back to the entrance.'

Posh eating was never my style. James had taken me out a couple of times, so had Jack, the millionaire but rough-edged owner of the amusement arcade, wanting to impress me, money no object. Maeve's Café was more like home with freshly caught fish from one of her hunky fisherman friends or a three-egg omelette when I didn't have the energy to cook.

A waiter shook out the napkin and laid it across my knees. I nearly told him I was quite capable of doing that myself. Then he handed me the menu. It was miles long. There was so much to choose from. Some dishes were

marked with a discreet 'v' meaning vegetarian. I fixed on
Caesar salad and mushroom stroganoff. Joanna went for
more elaborate dishes. And she ordered a bottle of
Californian Merlot. I hoped it was for both of us.

By the time we'd ordered, the other passengers on table
seventeen were arriving. They were interesting people. A
kindly middle-aged couple called Ron and Flo Birley from
Guildford. This was their fourth cruise and they set about
giving us a detailed description of the other three cruises
and all the places they had visited. It would be easy to get
along with them.

A tall, well-groomed man arrived, in a natty blazer, cravat
and pink striped shirt. Very dated. He bowed to all the
ladies, including me.

'Craig Quentin,' he said. 'I look forward to having the
pleasure of your company at this sitting each evening.
Quite delightful.'

'I'm Joanna,' said my employer, nodding politely. 'And
this is my friend, Jordan.' She gave no surnames, no clues
about anything. 'We're from Sussex.'

He didn't look like a Craig. He was probably a Colin or
a Brian and thought Craig gave a younger image. I scrutinized his face for signs of Botox. He had a normal quota
of wrinkles round twinkling eyes.

'Oh, what part?' asked Flo Birley. 'We often go there.'

'It's a big county,' said Joanna with a smile. 'You wouldn't
know our little corner.'

The last person to arrive was a large woman floating in
colourful chiffon. She wafted in, throwing waves of perfume
to each corner of the dining room. Her hair hung in white
waves, long earrings dangled their own music.

'Hello, hello, everyone,' she said. 'Sorry, I'm late. Got
lost on the way. I'm always getting lost. You'll find me in
the officers' mess tomorrow evening, I expect.' She laughed
heartily. I liked her. The waiter pulled out the chair beside
me for her. It creaked as she sat in it. She waved away the
menu. 'Bring me everything,' she said, grinning. 'I'm
starving.'

'Yes, madam –' he took the menu – 'a little of everything?'

'You know me.'

He obviously did. A regular cruiser. But I didn't think she would bore us with the details. She looked around the table with good humour.

'So who are all you lovely people?' she said. 'I'm Natasha, by the way, loads of accent. Some of my friends call me Nat or Tasha. I don't mind which. My father was pure Russian. My mother was a Slovakian dancer.'

I could feel Joanna shrinking by my side. She was wearing a classic pale blue trouser suit with silk half-buttoned shirt. It was as if all the buttons refastened themselves an inch closer, hiding the gold chains.

'I'm Joanna,' she said, cool as ice.

'And who are you, darling child?' said Natasha, turning to me. 'You look as lost in this big ship as I am.'

'Jordan,' I said, not feeling a darling child. 'This is my first cruise. I'm knocked out by everything. It's so big, so opulent.'

'As long as you're not knocked overboard,' she joked. 'We haven't got time for any sea rescues. All that having to stop and lower inflatable rafts and lifeboats. It takes ages. Holds us up for hours.'

'But they are trying to save a life,' said Joanna with a sniff.

'I say, let 'em drown,' said Natasha. 'If they are that stupid to fall overboard. The railings are high enough.'

The starters arrived and I was immediately fascinated by what everyone else had ordered. Every dish was decorated with squirls of this and that, carved carrot or radish, a leaf of dill. Even my Caesar salad had a couture look as if the walnuts were placed. Joanna had ordered three sorts of salmon in some fancy sauce. They were laid out in a pattern. I thought of rows of chefs in the kitchens (or were they galleys?) decorating hundreds of plates, going cross-eyed with concentration.

'So what do you do for a living, dearie?' Natasha asked me, her mouth full of grilled goat's cheese.

'Jordan doesn't work,' Joanna put in fast.

'Won the lottery, have you, dearie?' She grinned.

'Something like that,' I said, joining the game. If Joanna was going to create an air of mystery, I was all for it. 'Redundancy. The golden handshake.'

'Then the drinks are on you both,' said Craig, raising his glass with a wink. Let Joanna talk her way out of that one.

It was the most succulent of meals. I was bloated by the end, especially after being tempted by a three-chocolate mousse and cream. It was out of this world, dark, light and white. None of my new clothes would fit me if I went on eating like this. And drinking like this. I'd had at least two glasses of red wine. Joanna could hardly ration me when the waiter did the pouring. Perhaps he had sussed her out when she attempted to stop him with a hand over my glass which he pretended not to see.

'Are you going to see the show this evening, dearie?' asked Natasha. She was going to call me dearie for the whole of the cruise. 'It'll be spectacular if you like song and dance.'

'Well, Orpheus was supposed to be the greatest poet and musician,' I said, getting my bit of Greek knowledge in again. 'There's some mountain oaks standing somewhere in the pattern of one of his dances.'

This statement clarified my unique position at the table. I was simple-minded and should be treated with care and consideration. It suited me.

'The Olympus theatre, then,' said Joanna, declining coffee. 'Come along, Jordan.'

I nearly said, 'Yes, auntie.'

About four hundred songs later, I was out on deck. Joanna was fast asleep in her king-sized, gently snoring. I made sure that I had closed all the doors properly. We each had perforated door key cards, carried them with us at all times. I double-checked that I had mine. It would become a habit.

The night sky was amazing. All those stars winking and blinking way out there in the beyond universe, the waves rushing by. It was not cold. I had put on my leather jacket and let the wind blow my hair all over the place. After the strangest day, I was at last at peace.

I was aware of someone standing further along the rail. It was a ship's officer in uniform. He was medium tall, not like James, but with short dark hair and broad shoulders. I couldn't see his face properly as he was looking out to sea.

'Your first cruise?' he asked. Pleasant voice.

'Yes. How did you know?'

'You've got that gobsmacked look. Everything wonderful, so far?'

'It's true. I've never been on such a big ship. Never been on anything so lavish and luxurious. I live in two bedsits. Very frugal.'

He seemed taken back by my honesty. 'Then enjoy every minute. It's like Brigadoon, a different world, lost in space, a floating village. People don't even read the daily newspaper. The world outside doesn't exist.'

'We get a newspaper?'

'Delivered to your door. All the latest news, abridged.'

'Where are we?' I expected him to know. He was an officer.

'We've set a series of easterly courses through the English Channel. We'll be through the Dover Straits sometime after midnight. There are strong tides in the channel but we should maintain twenty-one knots.'

'How do you know so much?'

'It's my job to know.'

'And when shall we reach the Mediterranean?'

'The Mediterranean? We're not sailing south. Don't you know where you are going?' He looked amused and surprised.

'I thought all cruises went via the Mediterranean,' I said faintly. How stupid of me. I'd never looked up Norway on an atlas. Never had the time.

'Good grief, girl. We're going to Norway, to the Arctic Circle, to the North Cape and the midnight sun. Haven't you brought your thermals?'

'I've brought two vests.'

I was partially prepared. But prepared for what? That I didn't know. And I didn't want to know. I had a feeling that Joanna was keeping the worst from me. I shuddered at the thought.

'You'd better go in,' said the officer. 'You don't want to catch a cold.'

I smiled. I'd already been caught.

THREE

At Sea

The MV *Orpheus Odyssey* was sailing peacefully through the North Sea, no storms, no excessive ship movement, no alarming lurches. I was on deck, enjoying the fresh breeze after a large breakfast. Far too large for me. My banana on the run was a thing of the past. I'd had slices of mango, pineapple, melon, figs and mixed berries. Plus a slice of sweet seeded bread and a glass of tomato juice. I was packed to the gills, felt like a walking whale.

Many passengers helped themselves to a full English and their trays were piled with plates of bacon, scrambled egg, fried bread, mushrooms, baked beans, hash browns, toast, marmalade, Danish pastries, coffee. I don't know where they put it. Their legs must be hollow.

Joanna had managed to order room service, merely juice, a croissant and a rose. She waved me away. 'Go on deck, circulate, look around,' she said, removing cooling eye-pads from her eyes. 'Try to be normal.'

I bit back a retort. What sort of normal did she want? Standard, typical, conventional?

Three times round the promenade deck was nearly a mile, a brass plaque informed intrepid walkers. There were a lot of walkers in a variety of designer gear. I loved the great expanse of sea. No land in sight. I could have stayed on deck all day. Who needed lunch? Who wanted the early first sitting? Food was deported to lost causes.

Natasha joined me on my walk. She was wearing bright green pyjamas and a sort of flowing kaftan. Her clothes were beyond description but her smile was genuine and pleasant.

'Ah, Jordan, dearie. Walking down a large breakfast?'

'Walking down a small breakfast. I've never seen so much

food. I mustn't think of the starving millions in Africa and the Sudan. It would be too upsetting.'

'It doesn't do to think of the rest of the world while you are on board ship. Be thankful that you have this oasis of time in which to enjoy yourself. Pretend it's Brigadoon. The Sussex coast might be flooded next winter and you'll be holed up in a refugee camp.'

How did she know I came from Sussex? I'd said nothing to give her a clue. Maybe it was a chance remark and not aimed at me. That officer had mentioned Brigadoon.

'Sussex, Essex and Norfolk, too,' I elaborated. 'It's all low-lying land. It could be flooded any time. Wasn't there a terrible flood in 1957 when a lot of people drowned?'

'Canvey Island,' she said. 'It was disastrous. Water simply poured through houses, sweeping everything away. Fifty people died.'

'Not likely to happen in Norway,' I said, trying to steer the subject into safer waters. 'All those deep fjords.'

'Deep fjords are very dangerous,' she said, her hair flying in the breeze, white strands whipping across her face. It looked dyed, now that I was viewing the roots. Some of the warmth seemed to have gone from her eyes. 'They are cold because of the glaciers melting into them. Icy water. You could die in minutes.'

'I'll remember that when I go swimming,' I said.

She gave me a sharp glance. 'Keep your clothes on, girl.'

She left me in a flapping swerve, pushing open one of the heavy doors and disappearing inside, into the warmth and safety. I was stunned for a moment. There was obviously another side to the bubbly Miss Natasha. Come to think of it, her surname was a mystery. She had kept that to herself.

I took a cup of coffee from the cafeteria and sat on the stern deck, reading the *Orpheus Odyssey Now* programme of the day's events. Every minute of the day was scheduled with some activity to keep everyone busy. Deck quoits, shuffleboard, whist, bridge, lectures, art, craft work, port lectures, line dancing and ballroom dancing. The word relaxation was not evident. We were to be kept occupied. Boredom was banished.

I wondered what Doris and Mavis would make of all this. They'd probably have a whale of a time, trying everything, tracking from one activity to another. I couldn't even make up my mind.

'So there you are,' said Joanna, sitting beside me with half a cup of black coffee. 'I wondered where you had got to. You are supposed to be with me all the time.'

'But you told me to go on deck. Remember? I could hardly share your breakfast in bed,' I said.

'You've had plenty of air now,' she said, finishing her coffee. 'Let's go shopping.'

The shop was like a mini-department store. It sold everything. It was a walk-though store with display windows port and starboard. It was called Sheherazade, slightly mixing the Greek theme with Arabic. It sold everything from jewellery, make-up, to perfumes and expensive evening wear. Joanna spent a happy hour trying on sparkly sequinned tops of which I'm sure she had a dozen already.

'Captain's cocktail party this evening,' she said. 'Must have something new for that.'

Sure, the captain was going to notice her something new at a party for 600 passengers? It was a palm-pressing occasion, probably free drinks and canapés. No names, merely a sea of faces, passengers having their photos taken with the captain to show the grandchildren.

'Is it wise to go to such a big occasion?' I said. 'There will be hundreds of people there and you won't know who they are or who they might be.'

A flash of apprehension crossed her face, then she straightened her jacket. 'Well, that's your job. You could check the guest list.'

'They are hardly likely to mark the list with character ratings. Even if I am allowed to look at the passenger list. And I doubt it. Probably classified.'

'All the officers will be there to protect me. Safe as houses, as long as you keep closely by my side. Have you

got something suitable to wear? I hope you are not going
to embarrass me.'

'Oh no,' I said. 'Doris, my personal shopper, chose the
perfect outfit. I'm sure you'll be agreeably surprised.'

'Let's have lunch now,' she said, paying for her purchase
with her cruise card. She had bought a black sleeveless top,
embroidered with sequins and black roses framing the neckline. It was a cashless and childless ship. Every purchase
from the shop or a bar went on an account and was paid
for at the end of the cruise.

We lunched in the dining room. I would rather have picked
at some lettuce in the cafeteria on the lido deck, but no
trays and self-service for Joanna. She wanted silver service
and bowing and smiling and a napkin flicked over her lap.

It was an excellent lunch but I was not hungry. I cut
down on the courses, having only soup and salad. The ginger
ice cream was delicious but it brought home memories of
ice cream at Latching, all the cafés along the front, especially Marconis and their twenty different Italian flavours.
Although the ship was luxurious, I already wanted to go
home. An odd sort of homesickness. Twenty hours afloat,
surrounded by sea and I'd done enough cruising.

Joanna was chatting away to a new set of passengers at
the table. You could sit anywhere at lunch time. I had
forgotten how to talk. It was as if my tongue was para-
lyzed with food, glued to the roof of my mouth with
seasoning. Joanna didn't notice my quietness.

'I'm going to play bridge after lunch,' she said brightly.
'You can come along.'

'I'll bring a book,' I said.

The library was well stocked with a huge choice of books.
I chose a couple and hurried to find the bridge room which
was called No Deal. Someone had a sense of humour. I
found a quiet armchair in a corner and settled down. A few
glances were tossed in my direction as if my non-playing
presence was going to disrupt their bidding.

'Got my camera,' I said, patting my hip pocket.

It was a good book called *The Long Kill* by Reginald
Hill about a lone assassin whose eyesight was letting him

down and he was starting to miss his targets. I was fascinated by the detailed mechanics of rifles and shooters. I wondered if such a trained assassin might have his sight on Joanna Carter and would aim from a passing ship. It was a disturbing thought.

I was deep in the story when suddenly there was a short cry from the table where Joanna was sitting. She stood up, hands fluttering nervously at her shirt.

'Four times,' she cried out. 'Four times I've been dealt the ace of clubs, the death card. Who is it? Who's doing this? I demand to know who it is. I can't stay here a minute longer. It's too dangerous. Jordan, where are you?'

'I'm here,' I said, reluctantly putting a scrap of paper in as a bookmark. Did the black trefoil symbol represent death? Joanna would get a reputation at this rate. It would go round *Orpheus Odyssey* that there was a woman on board who thought the bridge room was dangerous.

I took Joanna to a bar where she ordered a large brandy. I put *The Long Kill* under my armchair, hardly a reassuring title. The colour was beginning to come back into her face. A steward hovered nearby, spotting immediately when her glass was empty and she ordered another. He returned with a second brandy and a glass of water for me, clinking with ice.

'Thank you,' I said, surprised. I hadn't ordered.

'Air conditioning,' he said. 'You need plenty water.'

But Joanna barely gave me time to drink it before she was off to the port lecture. We were due to arrive at Stavanger tomorrow and she wanted to know all about it. I'd never heard of the place. Call me ignorant. There was a Norwegian travel book in my shop which I should have brought with me.

'Stavanger is the largest port in the south of Norway,' the port lecturer began. Earlier that day she had been selling excursions in the tour office. Same woman, different hat. I had a feeling that this lecture would be less about history and more about selling tours.

It was a sales pitch but it was also interesting and saved me reading a brochure. It looked a quaint place with steepled wooden houses along the front and cobbled streets. It also had an old area which had survived some awful fire, and all the houses were built of white wood and formed part of a heritage centre.

'I'm going to get ready for the captain's cocktail party,' Joanna announced. 'I've a hair appointment first. Are you coming with me?'

'To the hairdresser's?'

'You are supposed to be with me, morning, noon and night,' she said sharply. 'And that includes the beauty salon. That's what I pay you for.'

'Fine,' I said cheerfully. I had a good book. It seemed that the written word would save me from Joanna overload. I decided to keep a detailed note of everything we did together and where we went, date, times, etc. It might be important to check times if anything happened to Joanna. If my employer questioned my attention span, I'd produce my little black book.

The Beauty Box salon was the place to be comfortably spoiled. Lots of silver chairs, pale pink walls, flowers and good lighting. I found a spot where I could watch Joanna and read fifty per cent of the time.

A pretty young woman came up to me with a trolley laden with jars and bottles. 'Would madam like a manicure while she is waiting?'

'No, thank you,' I said. 'I'm waiting for my friend. She's having her hair done. The lady over there.'

'I have no appointments. It would be complimentary, my pleasure.'

Now that was different. She could tell from my face that I was tempted. She brought over a small table on which was a bowl of soapy water and a pyramid of towels.

'Please,' she said, persuasively. 'Good practice for me.'

I closed my book. 'Go ahead. Practise.'

She told me her name was Leila and she was from Mumbai, the Indian port that used to be called Bombay. It would be six months before she went home to her family. She had two small children. Her husband had been killed in a motorcycle accident so now she was the chief provider.

But she did not sound upset about the unfairness, accepted that this was her fate, to be doing my nails.

She soaped and soaked my nails, filed and trimmed the cuticles, massaged my poor aching hands (all that holding a heavy book) and finally painted each nail a luscious deep plum colour, adding gloss and a fixative.

'With your hair colour,' she said, referring to the tawny mass tied back with a crinkle band, 'you must never wear pink.'

'I'll remember that. Thank you, Leila.'

I wanted to give her something, nothing so condescending as a tip. We didn't use money. 'Thank you,' I said again. 'My nails look beautiful. One day I will do something for you.'

She smiled and began clearing away the debris. She didn't know that one day I would keep my promise.

The captain's cocktail party began with two long queues of passengers dressed in their best, women in long evening or cocktail dresses, men in dinner jackets or kilts, waiting to shake the captain's hand, have their photo taken, get their free drink. Two queues were on either side of the Olympus theatre, one shuffling towards the captain and the other towards the staff captain.

Captain Brian Armitage had the longest queue. I felt sorry for the staff captain's lack of popularity and at the last moment skipped across the lobby to be introduced to him. Joanna would have no one less than the captain.

Joanna had barely glanced at my dress, probably dazzled by her own gown, sewn shoulder to hem with white sequins. Doris had spotted my dress in a charity shop, black chiffon lined with silk, hanging on a back rail among the small sizes. It had narrow shoulder straps and fish tail hem with ruffles, made for a shorter woman. It was a moral dress. I could barely move in it. But the skirt was beautiful and I loved the way it was cut on the cross and fanned around my ankles.

'Ah, the stargazing lady,' said the staff captain. It was the officer I had met on deck. He hadn't grown any but he looked very smart in his dress uniform, lots of gold braid. In the brightly lit theatre I could see that his eyes were a warm brown, not the icy granite of my James. My James? How could I claim the man to be mine? He was miles away, solving Yorkshire crime, occasionally sending a curt email.

'Hello,' I said. 'I didn't know you were someone special.'

'Staff captain, and I sometimes steer the ship. One-handed,' he grinned.

'Isn't it computerized these days?'

'Computers break down. Then it's hand signals.'

'I thought I felt a wobble.'

'That was when I spotted you from the bridge, stargazing.'

I almost spilt the drink in my hand. It was a sparkling white wine, not exactly champagne, but near. James never flirted. It was not his nature. He sometimes teased me or took a rise out of me. But flirt? It was a foreign accomplishment. Officers probably flirted a lot. Perhaps they were trained to flirt with female passengers.

'Always wear sunglasses,' I said, moving on out of danger.

I felt his glance follow me before he turned his attention to greeting the next party guest. I'd had my turn. There were so many people. So many lovely dresses. The floor must be awash with dropped sequins.

As I moved into the crowd, looking for faces that I knew, I heard a commotion from the far side. Something was happening. I saw a flash of blonde hair, a head that I had last seen being roller brushed and teased into a sleek helmet shape.

It was Joanna, shouting and screaming, her face distorted. I moved fast across the room. No time for hand signals.

FOUR

Joanna's diamond necklace had gone. She was clutching her throat where the gems had sat, her face pale and anguished.

'My diamonds,' she shrieked. 'I've lost my diamonds. Someone has stolen my necklace.'

I vaguely remembered her necklace, but among all the white sequins the necklace had been eclipsed. She had a jewellery box locked in the wardrobe safe and made mysterious trips to it. My safe contained my passport and a paltry wad of fivers and tenners for end of cruise tips. I was starting to wonder if I had brought enough.

'Are you hurt?' I asked.

'Do I look hurt?' she snapped. 'Someone has stolen my necklace.' She turned to the captain. 'What are you going to do about it?'

Captain Brian Armitage drew her aside. 'I'm really sorry, Mrs Carter. Are you sure you were wearing it? On such a beautiful outfit, you may have forgotten?'

'Of course, I'm sure I was wearing it. I'd never go to a cocktail party without my diamonds.'

He nodded. He never argued with passengers. 'I'll get the security officer to come and see you.' He moved away and switched on his mobile phone, his voice too low for anyone to hear.

'Aren't you going to search all the passengers?' she demanded.

'I hardly think that would be diplomatic,' he said. 'Maybe it has dropped to the floor. I'll ask the staff to make a thorough search. Clasps do have a way of coming undone or breaking. My wife is always losing things.'

What a smoothie. Full marks for the way he was handling the situation.

She turned on me angrily. 'You weren't here,' she said.

'You should have been watching, instead of going over to the other line.'

'I was checking those who had already arrived,' I said. I was beginning to catch on to her game and had rehearsed a few answers. 'Just to make sure.'

This was ridiculous. To make sure of what? Checking who? Knives up a kilt? Hatpins in an evening bag?

'Well, that's all right then,' said Joanna, taking another gin and tonic from a passing tray. 'We'll wait until the security officer gets here. Perhaps we'll get some action then. He might be more efficient than you.'

The most awful sense of foreboding loomed into mind, like an iceberg homing in on the *Titanic*. I don't know what made me think of him. I hadn't thought of this man for years. I had worked for the West Sussex police in the Criminal Justice department, dealing with the prosecution process, conviction service, court liaison and the dozens of other admin things which go on behind the scenes.

To alleviate the boredom, I read everything. And it was during this reading I discovered that a certain Detective Inspector Geoff Berry had let a vicious rapist walk free due to his recording incompetence. I made an official complaint through the correct channels.

The correct channels were not amused and I was suspended and eventually asked to leave.

OK, it was one door closing and another opening and I never regretted starting First Class Investigations. I'd solved a lot of crimes, some minor which might otherwise have been overlooked and never solved, and I'd met a lot of people. And I'd found James. A man who rarely showed his feelings.

DI Geoff Berry was the last person I wanted to see and here he was striding through the cocktail party in a well-pressed khaki uniform, lots of braid and brass buttons, cap tucked under his arm as if on parade. He didn't look pleased to see me, but returned his face to one of non-recognition in an instant.

'Captain Armitage?' he said.

'Ah, Berry. This lady, Mrs Carter, says her diamond

necklace has been stolen or lost, here at the party. Perhaps you'd like to take some details. I have my other guests to attend to.'

'Of course. Would you come this way, Mrs Carter, and tell me all about it.' He indicated some armchairs on the fringe of the party, well away from the bar and the circulating food.

He still had that mean look. Thin-lipped mouth and shifty eyes. I wouldn't trust him with a parking ticket. I'd never followed his career. Grapevine had it that he'd been moved to another station, some far-off place, not the Outer Hebrides, but nearby. On reaching retirement, lots of ex-police took security jobs. DI Berry had landed one on cruise ships.

Joanna refilled her glass from another passing tray. She had quite a thirst. 'I'm so glad you're here,' she said, touching his arm for support. 'I'm really upset. That necklace was given to me by my late husband. It's really beautiful.'

For late, read ex? I thought she was divorcing him. Or perhaps there was another previously unmentioned spouse, already laid to rest.

'A beautiful necklace for a beautiful woman,' he said.

Creep.

'This is Jordan Lacey, my companion,' she said, waving me to another seat. I had been down-moted from friend to companion. Perhaps she found *friend* difficult to say. Companion implied paid.

Geoff Berry barely glanced at me. He was getting a small notebook out of his top pocket. It looked new and unused. There was very little crime on board.

'Perhaps you'd like to tell me what happened. What time did you put the necklace on? Can you remember your activities in the last hour or so? Did anything unusual happen?' He sounded so like a policeman.

His interviewing technique had certainly not improved. He was aware that I was listening and an extra crispness came into his laconic voice. I had never liked him and I liked him even less now. He rambled on.

Joanna was a fraction on the merry side now, despite the

loss of her diamonds. I lost count of how many gin and tonics she had drunk. The party was almost over, stewards clearing up, passengers drifting off to first sitting dinner. But she was still sitting by the window, the sea rushing alongside at a lower level, rambling on about her jewels and her husband and recurrent depression. At least she didn't blurt out about the threats to her life and my reason for being on the cruise. She had that much sense left.

I knew I looked knock-dead gorgeous in the black chiffon, my hair piled up in a careless tumble. My nails looked good too. So I let him have an eyeful of my expensive outfit as I got up and encouraged Joanna to do the same.

'The first sitting bell has just gone,' I said. 'And it's time for us to go and leave the search in the capable –' I paused after the capable, to let him know I hadn't forgotten his incompetence – 'hands of Officer Berry.'

It made him sound as if he were on the beat again. This was not the way to make friends and influence people. There might be a knife in my back along a dark deck.

'Yes, yes,' said Joanna, with the slightest slurring. 'Capable hands.'

'Come along.'

'Nursemaid?' said Geoff Berry, in an aside. 'Is that your present role? Suits you, Lacey.'

'It implies a caring nature,' I said.

Joanna clung to my arm as if we were on lifeboat drill and on our way to lifeboat number ten. She was definitely the worse for wear and tear. I was sorry about the necklace but I'd never had any real jewellery. Even James had never given me anything and we had become close at times.

'It's worth thousands,' she flung back as I guided her out of the Olympus theatre towards a lift to the Delphi dining room. I didn't think she could manage the sweep of curving stairs to the lower deck. A trip would be disastrous. And I might get blamed.

'I'll make a note of that,' Geoff Berry said, opening his notebook again. At least he could still write.

Joanna slumped into a chair at our dining table and the waiter immediately poured her a glass of ice cold water.

I nodded my thanks but he was going round the table with the same intention. I don't think I'd had more than half of my glass of low vintage bubbly. I was very sober.

Some time later I left Joanna in the Olympus theatre, now transformed back from cocktail party to being a theatre, watching a late night revue. It was good. But I wanted to get away. I had been chained to her for the best part of the day and the cuffs were beginning to rub.

I grabbed my scarlet pashmina and wrapped myself in the warm folds. There was already a coolness on deck. We were nearing Norway, country of fjords and snow and glaciers. I had never given Norway a thought before. All I knew about it was that Norway was occupied during World War Two by the Germans and there had been an active underground resistance. Many books had been written about their courage and heroic exploits.

No time to go to the cinema. The last showing of a film had already begun, but then I wasn't on board to enjoy myself. I was here to steer an alcoholic female from one show of hysterics to another. Then I thought of the money in the bank and decided it must be worth it.

'Stavanger tomorrow,' said a voice I recognized. It was the staff captain that I had bumped into twice. He sounded tired and reminded me of James. Perhaps he'd had to steer the *Orpheus* while the captain wined and dined his table. Both sittings.

'What's Stavanger like?'

'Clean and pretty. No litter anywhere. Harbour water so cool and clear and blue with reflections. You might see swans with little cygnets paddling after their parents. It's walking country, everywhere in Stavanger. Norway is magical with spectacular mountains. You're going to love Norway.'

It was not the sort of reply I expected. He sounded like a poet. An officer on a cruise ship who thought like a poet? No, it couldn't be possible.

'I'm Jordan Lacey,' I said.

'I know,' he said.

'You know?' What was going on? How did he know?

'I looked you up. Officers are allowed access to the passenger list. I know you are travelling with Mrs Joanna Carter and have communicating staterooms. Rather unusual. You must be important or very wealthy.'

'I'm neither,' I said, but refusing to elaborate. 'So who are you?'

'I'm Staff Captain Hamish Duncan, one step down from the captain. But still learning. An apprentice captain.'

I was impressed. Still learning was a modest admission.

'We don't want any practice steering on this cruise,' I said. 'Mrs Carter will demand the best.'

'I am the best when the captain is asleep or entertaining.'

We had begun to walk along the deck and that was pleasant in a vague, no-stress way. No one else was about. It was too windy. There was a moon lurking somewhere in that clouded sky but very few stars. It might rain tomorrow.

'So why are you cruising with Mrs Carter, a lady who has assorted problems, I understand? I won't mention the diamond necklace or the bridge table.'

Word spread fast. I didn't know exactly what he had heard.

'I don't know what you have been told,' I said. 'But I am Joanna Carter's paid companion, or friend, depending on what mood she is in. It's two weeks out of my life when I have to concentrate on her safety but I do have another life.'

'Her safety?'

Mistake. That word had slipped out. I was beginning to feel tired. 'No, I meant her welfare, making sure she has everything she wants.'

'Enough gin and tonics?'

I laughed. That would do. If everyone on board thought I was looking after a recovering alcoholic, the easier it would be for me to assume that role. DI Berry might be right with his snide nursemaid remark.

'And double brandies,' Hamish Duncan went on. 'I've seen her bar account. She's way ahead of everyone in the consumption stakes. We'll have to call in somewhere to replenish stock.'

'Oh dear. I'll have to watch her ashore.'

'Don't worry, the Norwegian prices will put her off buying alcohol ashore. They are sky high.'

'Can we talk about something else?' I said. 'This is my time off.'

'Would you like a drink somewhere?'

We both laughed. It was not what he meant. He meant shall we go somewhere and sit down and talk but it had to be couched in other terms. He leaned on a rail and stared down into the dark, rushing sea. The ship was gathering speed. The power was there, the throbbing, the pulse, a great floating machine thrusting forty-three thousand tons of steel through the waves.

'Sorry, wrong thing to say.'

'But walking is fine.'

'Let's walk then. Are you warm enough?'

'Yes, thank you, staff captain.'

'Call me Hamish.'

It was easy to talk to him. We talked about everything and nothing. He didn't ask any probing questions about what else I did for a living or my status. He took it for true that I was a paid companion. It was not unusual aboard ship. Older people liked cruising. It reminded them of their youth when they could travel and see the world without a stick or a Zimmer frame. They often brought a carer.

'Do you ever get any time off?' Hamish asked.

'I don't really know. I'm expected to be at her beck and call, day and night. Maybe if she's having a facial or having her hair done, I might be free.'

'I get some shore leave. It would be fun to show you around. Norway is a beautiful country. You'll love it, even when it's raining.'

'Does it rain a lot?'

'It rains a lot. The port of Bergen has become a verb, meaning to rain.'

Some passengers were coming out on deck. That meant that the stage show was over and they were catching some air before retiring for the night. That also meant that Joanna Carter would be prowling around, looking for me.

'I'd better go,' I said. There was a bar at the entrance to the theatre. She might have stopped there, having a nightcap.

'Back in harness?'

'Something like that.'

'This is my mobile number if you ever need to talk to someone,' he said, writing it down on a card. 'Of course, I could be steering the ship through some tricky fjord but I'll always find time to rescue you.'

'I could help with the steering. I once had a rowing boat,' I said, putting the card in a safe place. I had a feeling I might need a friend one day. I must try to memorize the number. 'Thank you, staff captain.'

'Hamish.'

'Hamish.' It was difficult to say. I'd been saying James for so many years, it seemed disloyal to say another man's name.

Joanna was propping up the bar. She had a double brandy in front of her and did not seem to notice that I had been absent. There was hope for me yet.

'Did you enjoy the show, Jordan?' she said, all smiles. Her lipstick had vanished and the careful hair was losing its shape.

'Brilliant,' I said.

'That nice security officer says he's sure he'll find my necklace. All diamonds you know, worth thousands.'

'What a relief,' I said.

'Someone stole it. Took it off my neck without my noticing. So easily done in such a crush. I told the captain that there were too many people. He should have smaller and more select parties. Not invite everybody in sight. After all, not everyone is interesting. Not every single passenger on the ship deserves an invite. Like some media circus.' She was getting carried away.

The ever attendant barman came up to me. I didn't really want anything. 'A glass of tap water,' I said. 'I'm sorry but that's all I should like.'

'Ice, madam?'

He served it with as much aplomb as serving the most expensive drink. That was style. He looked at my nails.

'Leila did them,' I said.

'She good worker,' he said. 'Nice lady but lonely.'

'What are you talking about?' Joanna interrupted, propped on her elbows. 'What are you saying?'

'The Beauty Box, where you had your hair done this evening. We were talking about the staff there.'

'It was so slow,' said Joanna, draining her glass. I had no idea what she was drinking now. Double vodkas with lime? 'I was there ages. Still, my hair does look great. I was pleased and it was perfect for the captain's cocktail party, even if my necklace was stolen.'

'It could be lost,' I put in.

'Rubbish. That clasp was checked by the jewellers before I came away. I'd had it cleaned. Still, it is insured. I shall claim as soon as we get back.'

Small bells rang. I'd heard this all before somewhere but I couldn't remember where. Some other investigation. Was it an early case of Alzheimer's? Don't give me any tablets, doctor. Don't resuscitate. Just let me go.

The loss of James suddenly hit me straight between the chest muscles. That awful time when I thought I had lost him. It was a physical pain. I wanted him so badly. I had thought, for a blissful moment a few months ago, that he was mine, but he had slipped away again, like a silvery fish. No fishy smell. Only the tang of his aftershave and the sharp feel of his cropped hair under my fingers was enough to quicken my senses. He filled every corner of my life. He filled a milky, silky stillness that was impossible to describe.

'Are you awake, Jordan? I feel like dancing. Let's find a band that is still playing. There must be one somewhere.'

Dancing? Could I call this overtime?

FIVE

I t's called landfall. A local pilot came aboard in the early hours, long before anyone in their right mind was up and on deck, to steer the *Orpheus Odyssey* through the passage of Byfjorden. The ship was manoeuvred into the harbour.

Hamish told me he swung the ship over 180 degrees before coming astern on to the berth. I don't know why he told me these technical things. The first lines went ashore and the ship was fast by eight a.m. It was a foreign language but I was learning. All I knew was that *Orpheus Odyssey* was tied up alongside a dock that was surrounded by brightly painted houses and cafés.

It was sunny with only a few clouds and a light breeze. Where was this famous Norwegian rain? It was supposed to be drenching the place by the bucket load. The harbour water was clear and smooth with hardly a ripple. Swans and their cygnets were reflected in the water, just as Hamish said.

A message came to the room that the necklace had been found. And found in a most unexpected place. In a towel by the pool, among the crumpled towels, on its way to the laundry. In celebration, Joanna booked an excursion and we waited in a lounge for our coach number to be called and to be escorted to the dockside. It was all very smoothly organized but there was a lot of waiting. I started to get itchy to move, wanted to get off. One of the stewards was entertaining the tour operators with sleight-of-hand tricks, balancing a coin which disappeared, swallowing it, then making it reappear on the back of his neck. He must have practised for hours.

Stavanger was a clean and pretty place. Not a scrap of

litter anywhere. Even the younger generation put their litter tidily into bins. When I thought of Latching's sour streets, the littered sea front promenade and the daily dumping of fast food wrappers, cans and bottles, plastic bags, it made me shudder.

Joanna was hiding behind big dark glasses. They hid nothing but the expression in her eyes. Her hair alone was a landmark.

'We are going ashore,' she said. 'Keep close to me. I don't trust anyone.'

We piled on to a coach waiting at the quayside, fastened our seat belts, signed a form giving name and cabin number. Joanna tried to write illegibly. The guide introduced himself, rambling on, but I was too busy to listen. There was so much to look at, the new world outside. This country was fascinating.

'This was the country of the Viking warrior, King Harold the Fair-Haired. The Old Norse name was Stafangr and it was founded in 1125,' began the guide, a short man who leaned heavily on a stick.

The coach took us through a long tunnel under a fjord. It was pretty claustrophobic. Joanna began to get nervous. The guide pointed out a large hotel that was called Under Arm by the locals because it looked like a deodorant tube. We saw a monument of three swords in the ground by a lake which was about not wanting to fight any more. The fields were full of white plastic bags of grass which the Norwegians called troll eggs. They obviously have a good sense of humour.

Joanna was tiring. She yawned. 'How much longer is this going on? His voice is sending me to sleep.'

'Look, Joanna, there's a huge strawberry farm. And they found an old Junkers in the fjord over there. And we are only one and a half hours away from the ski slopes. Apparently they use roller blades to train for skiing.'

I was parroting the guide. The views were beautiful, fjords and hills and islands of trees. There were sea houses with water right up to their lower storeys so they could offload straight from ships.

He pointed out 'cleaning-up straights' where farmers used to change clothes before going to church. Joanna was nodding off as the guide's voice drifted in and out of her ears.

The coach returned to Old Stavanger through the preserved white houses that dated back to the eighteenth and nineteenth centuries. One hundred and seventy-three were saved from the disastrous fire that swept through the old town, and they were now a National Heritage site.

Joanna was asleep, hung-over by her night's drinking. I tried not to notice, to appear normal, but the other passengers kept glancing back, annoyed. She was mildly snoring.

'It's her medication,' I explained. 'Seasickness pills. They make you drowsy.'

They nodded, as if understanding.

We were back to the quayside in time for lunch. Joanna woke up. In time for lunch meant in time for a Pimm's Number One on deck in her schedule. We climbed the gangway and showed our swipe cards for an electronic check. Our bags were passed through a security scan but we had bought nothing.

'Take my coat to our stateroom,' said Joanna, heading for a deck bar. 'I'll see you in the dining room for lunch.'

I went straight on deck after taking her coat to the stateroom. No dining room for me, I was going to catch a salad in the lido cafeteria. It was buffet style so I could help myself to a little or a lot. But I was seduced by the choice and had spinach and ricotta cheese tortellini, then some rum ice cream and fruit salad. I would be as fat as a pig at this rate.

The afternoon excursions were assembling on the quay, ready to go.

There was some sort of commotion going on at the front of the ship. The pointed end. Passengers were leaning over the rail and peering down. Was it whales or dolphins? Hardly, we were still in harbour.

I scraped up the last fragment of sliced strawberry and hurried outside. They were looking down at the heaving water. It wasn't easy to see anything. Several women were turning away, their faces white with shock.

I suddenly thought of Joanna. Surely she hadn't jumped overboard? She was certainly depressed and acted unstable at times, especially after a few drinks.

Officers were coming on deck in droves and moving passengers away from the rails. Crew were rigging up screens and cordoning off the area. They were moving swiftly.

'Better not to look, miss,' one said kindly to me.

'What's happened?' I asked.

'Nothing for you to worry about,' he said.

'I'd like to know.'

'We'll soon sort it out.'

That kind of evasive answer got me really curious. I darted down stairs to a different deck, the promenade deck. The same sort of camouflage was being rigged up below. There wasn't a chance of seeing what was going on. But I did know it was something to do with the forward hull. I think I'd got the term right.

They could hardly be casting off as then the ship would veer away from her moorings, leaving a lot of passengers behind. They were winching down some sort of platform, probably a maintenance platform, which they used to paint the ship or clean portholes. *Orpheus Odyssey* was pristine white so she got painted a lot.

Craig Quentin was trying to peer round the rigged screens, his eyes bright with macabre curiosity, the way motorists slowed down to look at an accident. Did they really want to see a mangled body?

'It's a woman,' he said excitedly. 'She's caught up on some sort of emergency rope ladder. God knows how she got there.'

I didn't want to know. It sounded too awful. I turned away, not wanting to see. It was time to rescue Joanna from whichever bar she was chained to and steer her towards the dining room.

Chained to. The phrase had flashed into my mind. I began to hurry. I didn't like those kind of premonitions. Geoff Berry, the security officer, was also hurrying along the deck towards me. For once he wasn't looking supercilious or condescending.

'Jordan,' he said. 'I need to speak to you.'

I stopped politely but not politely enough to answer him.

'Are you travelling with Mrs Joanna Carter?'

'Yes, you know I am.'

'Is this her handbag?'

Now I am not the world's best advised on couture hand-bags, those costing hundreds of pounds with masses of straps and buckles and fancy leather. I buy my tiny shoulder bags from charity shops. A lipstick and a pen is all I need to carry about. And a notebook.

He was holding a carmine intrecciato bag, strips of leather intricately woven. I'd seen it only a few hours ago. Joanna had joyfully told me it was made by Bottega Veneta and cost over a thousand pounds. 'My favourite bag,' she'd said.

'Yes, I think so. I didn't know she had lost it.'

'She hasn't lost it. I've got it. I think you had better come with me.'

It sounded as if he was arresting me. But he couldn't arrest me, could he? This is a ship. He was not a police officer. But he hadn't lost the lingo.

'Where did you find the bag?'

'I am unable to disclose that information.'

'OK,' I said. 'Lead on. What's this all about?'

'You'll soon find out.'

'I think I'm entitled to know now,' I said. Geoff Berry brings out the worst in me. I can never forget how he got off with a transfer and I got suspended.

'You'll know in good time.'

We were going down and down staircases to the bowels of the ship. This was the metal-lined crew area, big bags of trash waiting to be unloaded ashore, stores coming in, stacks of unwanted luggage, the mortuary. No carpets on the metal floor. It was busy with stewards and waiters and crewmen. I saw Staff Captain Duncan in the distance but he didn't see me.

I followed DI Berry through a labyrinth of corridors, walls pasted with signs, announcements and warnings. I had no idea where he was taking me.

Then by the screens and activity around, I knew we were going towards whatever had happened.

'This way please, Jordan. Mind your head.'

I ducked down. A door in the side of the ship was open. One of those swinging platforms was close alongside. Someone lay on it, wrapped in a blanket like a butterfly cocoon. I recognized the light blonde hair and the head that rested on a pile of rope. It was Joanna.

A fresh breeze came in from the harbour water. I hung on to some rail.

'Is that Joanna Carter?'

'Yes.' It was a mumble, a whisper. I was stunned. 'Is she dead?'

'No, thank goodness, no. But we don't know what happened. She was strapped to a rope ladder, her feet almost in the sea. She's in shock. Maybe she will be able to tell us what happened when she comes round.'

'I'll look after her,' I said. I was stricken with guilt and remorse. I was supposed to be looking after her and instead I had gone to the lido café for a spinach and cheese tortellini.

'She's going straight to the medical centre. She needs to be checked out by the doctor. You can see her later. OK, lads, careful now. Bring her on board. Clear the way now.'

Berry was in charge. He made sure I felt superfluous, in the way.

'Thank you.' It was hard work getting those two words out. Not easy when I disliked him so. But I realized that somehow I had to get into his good books. It was a cruel lesson.

'I'll help you all I can,' said Geoff Berry, sensing a weakness in the defence walls. 'You can rely on me, Jordan.'

He left me abruptly, following the stretcher bearers. I didn't know where I was. I didn't know how to get out of this confusing network. I tried several service lifts but they didn't go to passenger areas. I was completely lost.

One of the uniformed Thai stewards took pity.

'I'll show you the way,' he said. 'Follow me.'

I followed him along corridors, up narrow stairs, through curtains, no idea where we went. But eventually we reached carpet. Carpet on the floor meant a passenger area.

'Thank you,' I said. 'You've been very kind. I hope I haven't delayed you.'

'No problem, miss.'

I didn't really know what to do. It was extraordinary. Joanna Carter had been found strapped to a ladder, half submerged. She was now in the medical centre, being checked out by their medical staff. I was unwanted on voyage.

But there was something I could do. I could trace her last steps, find out what had happened. Now, which was her favourite bar for Pimm's Number One?

She had half a dozen favourite bars. She would have gone to the nearest first. The barman remembered her, but she hadn't stayed. Joanna liked to circulate, cruising. As I went from bar to bar, I realized that she had drunk a lot of Pimm's before lunch. All the bar staff remembered her. She was a good customer.

'She was going to have lunch in the dining room,' said the last barman, polishing glasses. He didn't trust the glass-washing machine. 'She was looking forward to her lunch. She said she was meeting someone for lunch.'

Now that was news, unless she meant me. But she would hardly look forward to lunching with her paid companion. She must have picked up a date. After all, she was good-looking and a wealthy woman. Some men like women with money.

'Thank you,' I said. 'Have you any idea who she was meeting?'

'A gentleman, I think.' He shook his head. 'Can I fix you a drink? You look pale.'

'Thank you, but no. Another time,' I added, seeing his face drop.

The next stop would be the dining room. But it was closed. Lunch was over and the staff were having a well-earned rest before the mad session of two sittings for dinner.

I turned away from the flower-flanked wide glass doorway. It always looked so elegant. I bumped into someone. 'Sorry.'

'Jordan? Is that you, Jordan? I can't believe it. Hello?'

I knew the voice. Warm and kindly. I had known the voice for years. It went back a long time to Latching, with a lot of bad funfair memories.

'Francis Guilbert,' I said. 'Of all the p–people. I'm so glad to see you. Are you on this cruise?'

'Jordan, my sweet girl, of course, I'm on this cruise. How are you? Whatever is the matter? You look really upset.'

Then, of course, I did a most unacceptable thing. I burst into tears. And in moments, Francis had his arms round me and was patting my shoulder in a fatherly way.

He'd always been like a father to me. And now I needed him.

'I think you need a shoulder to cry on,' he said, leading me to a secluded area. 'Tell me what this is all about.'

It came into my head without thinking. 'It's called keel-hauling,' I said.

SIX

At Sea

F rancis Guilbert owned the biggest department store in Latching, a mega retailer. I had worked there once, as undercover staff, during a Christmas period of strange unexplained stock losses. I still had the black dress. The other loss was the tragic death of his son on a funfair ride. I'd solved both cases. Francis liked me, rather too much, but the age gap was more than I could cope with.

But he was here now on the Double O and I was pleased. Francis had a friendly face and a kind heart. The Gods had arranged this. It was more than I could have hoped for. Except James. He would have been perfect. This was near perfection.

'My dear Jordan,' said Francis, leading me away. 'Let me get you a coffee. You look absolutely done in. Are you on holiday? Or is this a case?'

'It's certainly a case now,' I said.

We went up the curving staircase to the deck above where there was a wall-long bar and lots of small tables and armchairs. We sat down and an attentive waiter was there in seconds.

'Two coffees and two brandies,' said Francis. He was still a handsome man with his thick grey hair and clear hazel eyes. He had a beautiful double-fronted old house in Latching and a thriving business, but no son to pass it on to now. I couldn't be a surrogate son.

'Jordan,' said Francis. 'I'm absolutely delighted to see you here on the *Orpheus Odyssey*. I hope it means you are having a well-earned holiday. And seeing some of the world. I know how much you love the sea. You're always walking Latching pier in all weathers.'

'It's not exactly a holiday,' I said. 'But I'm working,

acting as a bodyguard for a very nervous woman who thinks someone is out to kill her.'

'And are they?'

'I don't know. Maybe they nearly did. She is the passenger they have just found strapped to a rope ladder, almost under the keel. She's still alive. But it can hardly be classed as a deck game.'

Francis signed the chit for the drinks. 'Thank you, young man. But how awful, Jordan. No wonder you are shocked and in distress. Well, I'm here now. Always a reliable shoulder to cry on, and always another cluster of brain cells to help solve your mysteries. Though, sorry to say, the brain is working a little slower these days. There's still a job open for you at Guilbert's. I live in hope.'

I had to smile. He was such a sweetie. We'd had a lot of laughs together and many cold suppers in his big, empty house. Then Francis began to get serious, throwing hints about moving in, and how good we were together. But he was thirty years older than me. And I loved James. And always would. Even now, despite the calming brandy, I was itching to get to the Internet study and surf the air waves, sending James an urgent email.

Instead I told Francis about Joanna Carter and her suspicions, her drinking and her paranoia. About me being hired to be her bodyguard. There wasn't anything I didn't tell him. Except I didn't mention the fee and my current urgent need for capital. He would offer to lend me the money and I wasn't having that. He nodded occasionally, taking it all in.

'My dear, you have done everything that you could, without being at her side every second of the day and night. There was nothing definite to go on. Her suspicions were vague. You mustn't blame yourself for what happened today. She was simply going to a bar for a drink and perhaps had one too many. It might have been a very stupid prank. First of all, you need the facts. So far you know practically nothing, beyond all the bars that she went to. At least Mrs Carter is still alive. Wait until she tells you what happened.'

'You're right. I need to know the facts.'

'Can the security officer on board help you?'

I groaned. 'I doubt it. We are not exactly buddies. Quite the reverse. He's the man I least trust in the whole, wide world.'

Francis didn't comment. He was wise enough not to push me.

I wasn't going into details. They were unprintable. My recall of that painful period was erratic. It depended on my roaring hormones. I could be stoic or on the verge of murder.

'I'll go and see the ship's doctor,' I decided. 'See if Joanna is recovering all right. That will be the first step.'

'And understandable,' said Francis. 'You'd be concerned for your friend. Would you like to join me for dinner this evening? I'll ask the restaurant manager to find us a quiet table for two. I'm sure you won't want to talk to a lot of people.'

I nodded. 'That's true. Thank you. First or second sitting?'

'I think it will depend on where he can fit us in. Give me your cabin number and I'll leave a message on your phone.'

He took the number of the stateroom and wrote it down on a slip of paper. It was a bridge score card. 'I'm having lessons,' he said with a grin. 'But I'm not very good at it. Bridge requires concentration and I keep looking out of the window.'

'Thank you for the drinks,' I said. I felt stronger despite the gnawing in my stomach. Cheese and spinach is hardly filling. I wondered if I could wait till dinner with Francis. I was becoming a food addict. It must be something they put in the drinking water.

The medical centre was way down in the depths of the ship. Perhaps they hoped that passengers would have recovered by the time they found the right deck and the right corridor.

It was like a mini-hospital with a receptionist, a waiting room, surgery, several small side wards and somewhere an operating theatre. Everywhere was antiseptically white and uncluttered. The receptionist wore white. The nurse wore white. The doctor, when he came out to see me, wore a

white jacket and white trousers. It was like something out
of a futuristic film.

'I'm Dr Max Russell,' he said, shaking my hand. 'You're
enquiring about Mrs Carter. Do I know you? Are you a
friend?'

'I'm Jordan Lacey, her travelling companion,' I said. 'We
are in A708 and A710 staterooms on A Deck. You can check
with the purser.'

I could hardly say I was her bodyguard and that I'd been
stuffing my face with rum ice cream while she was being
attacked. If she was attacked.

'Is she all right?'

He took me into his surgery and closed the door. 'Please
sit down, Miss Lacey. I'm sorry about the caution, but I
had to know who you were. Someone has caused this
appalling episode. The shock and fright are severe, and it
could be anyone on board. Everyone is under suspicion.'

'What exactly happened? You have to tell me. I can't
help Joanna if everything is surrounded in secrecy.'

Dr Russell was tall, tanned and rugged with an Australian
drawl. He was not handsome in a textbook way, not nearly
as good-looking as James, but he had the right sort of person-
ality to soothe irate passengers who wanted to sue every
member of the ship's company. It was a compensation
mentality these days and the first thing passengers wanted
as evidence was a doctor's certificate saying that they had
really suffered.

'Firstly, Mrs Carter is sort of all right. She is not injured,
nothing broken, no lost blood, a few minor cuts and bruises,'
he began. 'But she is in a bad way. We're treating her for
shock. Keeping her warm and quiet in a private room.'

'What do you mean, sort of all right? What happened to
her?'

Dr Russell pursed his mouth. 'We don't know. She
hasn't said a word. She isn't speaking. As far as we can
tell from the evidence, she was bound and gagged and
strapped to the forward keel ladder. It's an emergency
ladder used mainly for repairs. One of the crew spotted
her and so the rescue operation was activated. But as far

as I can make out, she hasn't spoken to anyone about what happened.'

'Perhaps she'll tell me,' I said, inwardly sinking. I was riddled with guilt. I should have been with her. I might have been able to stop this nightmare.

'That's a good idea. Would you like a cup of tea and a biscuit? You're looking a little pale yourself.'

'Yes, thank you,' I said, standing up. 'Could you show me the way?'

'I'll come with you.'

The doctor led the way along a corridor. There were lots of doors off the corridor and he took me to the last one. It was a plain and ordinary private room, with none of the stateroom luxury and comforts, apart from a decent bed and side table, and some pleasant modern pictures on the walls.

I would have felt quite at home in it. But I was glad I wasn't.

Joanna Carter was sitting bolt upright in the bed, minus her smart trouser suit, a duvet wrapped round her, her hair damp. She was staring ahead, her eyes fixed on some point above the door. There was a saline drip fixed into a vein in her arm.

'Hello, Joanna,' I said. 'It's Jordan. I've come to see how you are.'

She didn't move or even seem aware of my being there. I sat down on a chair and took her other hand. It was icy cold. Felt dry and papery.

'She's very cold,' I said.

'It's shock. The bed is heated,' said Dr Russell.

'Hello, Joanna. Talk to me, please. Say something. You don't have to tell us what happened, but we want to know that you are all right. Dr Russell here is worried about you. We are all worried about you.'

These were sincere words despite my not liking her. She looked dreadful. Her face was white, showing up make-up smears and mascara runs. The pupils of her eyes had blackened and there was no expression in them.

'She can see, can't she?' I suddenly panicked.

'Yes, there's no damage to her eyes. She's in a severe state of shock. Not surprising really. It must have been a terrifying experience, however she got there, almost in the water.'

A nurse came in with a tray of tea and biscuits. It was nicely laid with two cups and saucers, a teapot and milk jug. No NHS plastic and polystyrene.

'Perhaps you could persuade Mrs Carter to have some tea. She has accepted nothing from us. I'm afraid I have to leave you now. There are some patients waiting outside.'

'I'll stay with Joanna,' I said. 'I won't leave her.' It was a bit late to make that promise.

I sat with Joanna for over an hour. She never said a word and made no indication of being able to take the cup of tea. In the end I drank the tea and ate the biscuits. There was nothing I could do. I half expected her to suddenly pounce on me and tell me off for not being there when she needed me. But she never moved. She was like a statue, turned to salt, like Lot's wife.

'I've got your handbag,' I said. 'You know, the pretty red leather one. Would you like to do your hair or fix your face?'

I got out the small vanity purse she always carried around and opened it. There was the usual collection of lipstick, mascara, perfume. Something else dropped out. It was a small silver key. But it wasn't a luggage key or a safe key. I didn't recognize it at all.

Joanna's expression didn't change. I put everything back into the purse including the key. 'Well, it's here if you want it,' I said. People did this for coma victims. Talked to them endlessly for day after day or played their favourite music. Maybe this was my punishment. I'd be here in this small room, day after day, while the Double O cruised the fjords and the midnight sun. They'd make me up a camp bed on the floor. I wouldn't know if it was day or night.

The door opened and the nurse came in to take the tray. 'Dr Russell thinks you should leave now. It won't help if you become ill too. We'll look after Mrs Carter and there'll be an officer on guard outside her door. We are going to sedate her so that she gets some sleep.'

I got up stiffly. 'Thank you. I'll come back later.'

'Any time.'

I got into the nearest lift and pressed any button. It didn't matter which deck I went to, as long as I got some fresh air. The lift stopped at the promenade deck, my favourite. I set to walking a mile round. We were still in Stavanger, although I could see the last afternoon coach trips returning and passengers queuing up to come aboard. We must be sailing soon. I'd lost all track of time.

Such a pretty place. I had enjoyed the morning so much, looked forward to a stroll round the town after lunch, taking in the cobbled streets and all the ships and boats in the harbour.

Most of the passengers were laughing and chatting. Word had not spread of the incident. No doubt the ship's grapevine would be in action this evening. Meanwhile it was being played down. Hardly an item for tomorrow's daily newspaper.

Free. The word came into my head. I was free. Joanna Carter was being looked after by the medical staff. There was a guard on her door. All I need to do was pay regular visits and find out what I could. A burden rolled off me. But first I needed a shower.

The two staterooms looked the same, neat and tidy, clean towels in the bathrooms, bins emptied. A pail of fresh ice in the refrigerator. Our steward, Ali, had serviced the staterooms. Everything was spic and span.

Yet I had a feeling that someone had been in. Perhaps it was too tidy. Someone had looked around or had been searching for something. It was difficult to pin down this feeling but I knew it was so. It was intuition that crept along my skin, prickling, alerting my senses.

I picked up a heavy brass lamp and opened all the wardrobe doors, one by one. Heaven knows what or whom I expected to jump out at me. But there was no one hiding in the staterooms.

I went into locking every door mode before I took a shower. That *Psycho* film haunted me. Then I saw the blinking red light on the phone by my bed. There was a message from

Francis saying he'd booked a table for two at the second sitting.

The ship was moving. I went out on to the balcony in time to see her sliding away from the quayside. At first it was only a few inches, then the gap widened. The lines had been let go. The ship's hooter nearly made me jump out of my skin. It was the traditional naval goodbye to a port. Once clear, the ship steamed out of the harbour. I supposed we had a pilot on board, steering us through the home waters that he knew so well.

Second sitting meant a long gap between now and food. My stomach was hooked on food. I went to the Internet study and emailed James. I told him what had happened. Then I went on to Google and surfed keelhauling. It was a medieval form of punishment, pulling the victim under the keel of the ship. Joanna would have died on leaving Stavanger, as the ship turned round. It seemed a freak incident. But then so had my nun on a meat hook been a freak murder.

The wind was getting up. They cordoned off some of the outside decks. No one overboard on this cruise, please. I could hear the wind howling through the deck superstructure. Crew were hurrying about, securing deckchairs with yards of rope, collecting cushions, making everything safe. They were hooded and fastened into weatherproof navy anoraks.

It was not an evening for finery. It was coded semi-casual. I wore the black dress from Guilbert's store. The neckline was ribbon-edged and I had my crimson pashmina to throw over my shoulders. I would be warm and comfortable. I wondered if Francis would recognize it.

To ease my guilt, I made a lightning visit to the medical centre. They assured me that Joanna was sleeping now and there was no need to visit her till the morning. Guilt rolled off me like melting butter.

Francis was waiting for me outside the Delphi dining room. His semi-casual was, of course, a blazer, shirt and tie. He smiled, recognizing the dress.

'As lovely as always,' he said, forever gallant. 'I'm glad you still wear it.'

The table for two was well away from the crowds. I could not have borne being questioned by everyone we knew. Francis was the perfect host, ordering wine without consulting me. I didn't care what I drank. It wasn't cranberry juice.

Strangely, my rampant hunger had eased. A transitory thing. It was a delightful meal. I even made a few notes as I ate more than I ought to. I might never eat like this again.

Asparagus spears with hollandaise sauce, followed by cream of Stilton and leek soup, followed by a champagne sorbet. Wasn't that enough for any human? No, we were not even halfway. I felt tired just reading the menu.

I went for a small portion of baked fillet of halibut while Francis chose beef Wellington with Perigordine sauce. Whatever was that when you were at home? I couldn't count the veggies offered. At some point, I had to say, no thank you, no more please. I was sated with food.

The desserts were mouthwatering. Crème brûlée, chocolate and mint parfait, plums in sangria syrup. I went for fresh strawberries Romanoff. Did this mean they were Russian strawberries? Fortunately it was a small helping, decorated and dusted with icy swirls of this and that, like a picture on a plate.

Neither of us had an inch of room left for the cheese board or the fresh fruit or the petits fours.

'Coffee in the lounge, I think,' said Francis. 'Then these poor souls can start clearing up. Do you want to go to the late showing of the musical tonight? I've no idea what it is.'

I shook my head. 'I don't think so, Francis.' Suddenly I was tired out. I would check one last time on Joanna, then have an early night with a book. Or make some more notes. I was forgetting my cardinal rule. Write everything down, even the smallest detail. 'You've been so kind, Francis, and I've enjoyed your company. But I've a few things to do before I turn in.'

'I quite understand. A little sleuthing. Don't let me detain you.'

I dropped a light kiss on his cheek with a smile of thanks.

Francis was looking happy and content. Perhaps he was imagining a series of suppers for two.

I went back to the Internet study and keyed in my registration number and password. It was all very high tech. I was hoping for a reply from James. It flashed up on the screen that I had a new message. It was from a coded name I didn't recognize and the subject matter was business.

'Keep your nose out of this. It's none of your business,' it said. It wasn't signed. It was a direct warning. And someone who knew my email address. I felt vulnerable and hollow. Was I the next target?

SEVEN

Almost At Sea

I t had been a delightful day at Alesund, but I had only
been able to hop on and off the ship, not daring to be
away from Joanna for long. The town was a feast of Art
Deco houses with a lovely meandering canal to wander
along and as always, a range of majestic mountains in the
distance.

Preparations had been made to cast off but the movement of the ship was wrong. It wasn't the usual full steam
ahead, but a sort of erratic rocking. The word battering
came into mind. I had no idea if we were still berthed alongside at Alesund. The Double O had been scheduled to leave
at six o'clock in the evening, and as far as I knew, all the
passengers had returned safely.

There had been no urgent messages earlier, tannoying for
passengers Mr and Mrs So-and-So to pick up the nearest
phone and dial reception. The swipe card check occasionally hiccupped and the missing passengers were usually
found on board, in their cabin, in a bar, on deck, oblivious
of the mild panic on the bridge.

It looked windy outside the balcony. I could feel the ship
rocking more wildly. But I'd walked the Latching sea front
in winds far stronger than this. It was about force six, a
southwesterly, still overcast with occasional sweeps of rain.
But the Latching's sea front was solid and steady and a
deck balcony was not.

I pulled a track suit on and fastened a warm anorak. No
one else was on deck. That email still irked me but I refused
to be scared of an email. I'd had far worse in my days at
First Class Investigations. There had been all sorts of nasty
warnings through my letterbox.

There were land lights to starboard, twinkling in the hills.

We were still berthed at Alesund, despite my seeing a gap growing earlier. Had I dreamed that departure?

The wind was stronger than I thought and the Double O was being blown against the berth, despite all the sturdy lines holding the ship. There must be some worried faces on the bridge. She was a big ship and needed a lot of power to turn her against the wind.

Once she could head into the wind, she'd be off and away. But now she was sideways on, thousands of tons of white steel, the size of a tower block of flats.

They needed another tug. Even a novice like me could see that. Maybe a couple of extra tugs, powerful ones. Perhaps I ought to ring the bridge and suggest it. There was a phone number on display somewhere, that anyone was invited to ring if it was a man overboard emergency.

'Don't stay on deck, Jordan. It's too dangerous.'

Staff Captain Hamish Duncan was hurrying along the deck, done up to the chin in navy waterproofs. A gust of wind nearly knocked him against me. He caught hold of a rail to steady himself, inches from a collision.

'The wind is forty-five knots,' he said. 'You should go inside, Jordan. It isn't safe.'

'I want to watch what's happening,' I said.

'Not sensible. It's a difficult departure manoeuvre, but everything is under control. Go and watch a film in your stateroom.'

He looked anxious and I didn't want to add to his troubles. His dark hair was blowing about. It added to a general sense of disorder which gave me another feeling of alarm. The cruise brochures didn't warn passengers about dreadful weather. The photographs were always of sunshine on deck and happy people at a bar.

'You need another tug,' I said.

'Correct. A couple are on their way. You'll make a seaman yet.'

Supposing they couldn't move the Double O? Two weeks in Alesund wouldn't be that bad. It was a fascinating place with those mountains to explore and the seven nearby islands joined by ferries or tunnels.

I couldn't open the heavy door to the inside corridor, nor could I walk unaided to the next set of doors. Hamish added his weight and we managed to push the door wide enough for me to hurry inside. The wind was starting to howl.

The relief was instant. It was warm, calm and cut the wind, despite the rocking. I didn't want to go back to the staterooms. I didn't want to watch a film. I wanted to know what was happening. Hamish had already gone with some haste so he missed my smile of thanks.

Somewhere there was a late night bar, quite small, called the Bridge Bar. It had a panoramic window. I'd not been there before. Tonight there was a small cluster of passengers glued to the windows, watching the manoeuvres.

'Hello, Jordan.' A man detached himself from the group, whisky glass in his hand. It was Craig Quentin from our dining table. His company was not my first choice at any time although I could not pin down why. But I could hardly snub him in these circumstances. 'Spiffing fun, isn't it? We might be stuck here for weeks. Who cares, as long as the bar stays open?'

'Fun for us but not for the captain,' I said. 'He must be very worried.'

'They'll work it out. Probably the extra tugs they need are miles away, and it's taking hours to move them to this fjord. Can I get you a drink?'

It was a bit late for any more drinking but I accepted a pineapple juice. Craig raised a bushy eyebrow but ordered it from the bar. The barman was sleepy-eyed. It was getting late. He couldn't close until the last drinker left.

The wind was streaming through the ship's flags on line. They were flapping violently, being shredded. I hoped they had a stock of new ones on the bridge. The decks below were ghostly, shrouded in shadows.

I felt like a shadow myself. Talking to this man was not normal.

'Here she comes,' said Quentin, pointing to a sturdy ship shape that was emerging through the darkness. 'Help at last. A powerful, tough tug. She's going to be made fast centre, I bet. Lead aft.'

I wondered how he knew so much, but what was going on below was so interesting, I forgot about the man standing beside me. The tug looked small and squat beside the long, elegant Double O. She didn't look strong enough to tow a rowing boat.

'How will they do it?' I found myself asking.

'They'll use this new forward tug and the ship's thrusters to slowly bring the bow off the berth. The other tug, at the stern, will hold the stern off the dock, so we don't get banged against it. The new tug is going to have to work damned hard to swing the *Orpheus Odyssey* to the port. Tricky stuff. Once we are turned round, we'll be able to head out of the harbour, use the wind to our advantage. On our way to Trondheim.'

'How do you know all this?'

He tapped his nose. 'Years of cruising, m'dear. You pick up a few things on the way.'

Quentin was right although it seemed an age before the great ship began to heave and move. The forward tug was billowing clouds of smoke and we could see the strain on the heavy cables. I imagined the staff captain sweating it out on the bridge. He deserved every inch of the gold braid sewn on his dress uniform.

I was ready for sleep now that I could feel the reassuringly regular movement of the ship as she headed into the wind and out of the harbour. The pilot stayed on board for several hours, taking us through troubled waters. For a short while I had forgotten Joanna's plight and the warning email.

A small drama at sea. I could only endure small dramas.

'Thank you for the drink, Craig,' I said. 'Fascinating to watch. See you tomorrow sometime.'

'Goodnight, m'dear. Take care. There's still a lot of movement.'

Craig seemed settled in for a long night's drinking so I made my way down to the next deck. I could sleep now that everything was all right. Everywhere was deserted, not a soul anywhere. I was halfway down the staircase when there was a sudden violent push in the middle of my back. I gasped.

My feet lost their grip on the carpeted stairs. I felt myself falling, flying through the air in slow motion. My hand shot out to grasp the banister but my fingers were suddenly slippery with sweat and weak with fear. I felt the polished wood slide away from me as I tumbled.

We learned how to fall in the police force. Long forgotten training came automatically into my brain and transferred swiftly to my body. It's the landing that causes injuries, not the fall. Land hard and you'll break something. So land away from obstacles. Strike your head on an immovable object and that's trouble. That's pain and blood and stitches, maybe concussion.

I went into a roll. Just in time. I felt the hardness of the landing floor but let my body roll into the space. It knocked the breath out of me. I lay there, not moving, hoping that nothing was broken. In that moment I opened my eyes and looked upwards to the top of the stairs.

I thought I saw a shadow move away but I could not be sure. There was a small flash of light but I couldn't recognize its significance. But it hadn't been the wind that sent me flying. It had been a deliberate human punch. I'd been punched before, many times. There'd be a bruise in the morning.

EIGHT

Trondheim

I didn't break anything but I was as stiff as an ironing board the next morning. Rolling out of bed was the only option. A hot bath helped and I stayed under water until the prune effect took hold. So I had an enemy on board who sent me nasty emails and pushed me down the stairs. Not nice.

This bodyguard business was taking on a whole new aspect. I was unsure of anything, especially myself. I was still eating more than was healthy for anyone, although I kept hopefully to fruit and salad. It was the undercover extras that were piling on the weight.

People kept coming to me with theories about poor Joanna. It was kind enough but I didn't want to know how they thought Joanna got strapped to the rope ladder. I wanted to hear it from her own lips. But she was still not talking.

And the weather was awful. Forget a Caribbean tan. It was too cold and too windy to sit anywhere outside on deck. Take a sleeping bag or a rug and find a sheltered corner. Walkers on the promenade deck were wrapped into anoraks and scarves. The shop sold out of socks and gloves.

The ship was making slow progress. She felt heavier. We had all eaten too much porridge. The ship was entering the Trondheimfjord and proceeding towards the berth, guided by a pilot. It was a long way, some eighty-five nautical miles and still windy.

The crimson pashmina made a perfect scarf, folded long-ways and knotted round my throat. It was blissfully warm. I stopped worrying about Joanna. She couldn't come to any harm in the medical centre. My aim was to find out what had really happened and I couldn't do that if I was frozen to the deck in a torpor.

Joanna and I were booked to go on a city tour, so I decided to join the party on my own. I might pick up something from the passengers. They were more talkative when in smaller groups.

Staff Captain Duncan caught sight of me while waiting in the queue to disembark. Cruise life was turning into one long queue for this or that but don't tell anyone. 'A quick word?' he asked.

'Of course,' I said, stepping aside. It would have to be quick or I would get black looks from the passengers on the coach. Or left behind on the quayside.

'I thought you might like to know that we have additional ammunition in our investigations. A passenger who is a retired police detective, quite high ranking I think, has offered to help out.'

'Wonderful,' I said, not sure if I meant it or wanted interference.

'Would you like to meet him?'

My heart sank still further. 'Maybe . . .' I replied, unenthusiastically.

'I'll be in touch,' he said, ushering me back into the queue at a different point. I ignored the outraged expressions. After all, I had given up my original place in the line. People could be quite emotional about queues.

Trondheim was indeed a medieval city. I expected to see pilgrims and merchants, maybe even King Olav II Haraldsson himself, riding the streets on a great horse, clothed in furs and armour. The city had had its share of fires, fifteen in five hundred years, each time reducing the city to ashes. Somehow the great Nidaros Cathedral had survived, especially the spectacular west front with its rows and rows of stone statues of Norwegian kings and bishops. One bishop had three heads in a basket, apparently his nephews. I didn't want to know that story.

'This is the cathedral for all of Norway's coronations,' said our guide. This was news to me. I was so ignorant, I wasn't even aware that they had coronations.

The Royal Palace, built by a rich merchant's widow in

1774, was the biggest wooden building in the world with 140 rooms. Some scout hut. There were tavernas on poles and old warehouses on stilts striding the River Nidelva. A lot of water, canals and rivers, very picturesque.

But I liked the modern things too. Some bright spark had come up with the idea of a bicycle lift up the steep Brubakken hill, almost up to the Kristiansten Fort. An underground cable, operated by a key card, gently pulled the bike up the hill while the cyclist kept his foot on a footplate.

It looked a lot of fun. Anyone could have a go. Apparently the tourist office would let you borrow a bike and a key card and try it out. I'd have liked a go. But there wasn't time as our tour was hurried along to the next piece of historic architecture.

Even more to my liking was the flower bridge for pedestrians and cyclists. Each side was a riot of flamboyant pansies, all colours, planted in troughs on top of the stone ramparts. What a perfect memorial this would make for our sad princess. A flower bridge where daily people could walk and stroll over a river. Far better than a leaky pond in a park.

It was still trying to rain and the wind was gusty. Umbrellas were blown inside out regularly. They went into litter bins. No dumping them in gutters in Norway. My cap kept blowing off. By the time we got back to the ship, my hair was dripping wet.

I hurried aboard and down to the medical centre, hoping that Joanna had not been demanding my attendance. The receptionist offered me a towel. 'You don't want to drip all over her,' she said.

'Is there any change?'

She shook her head. 'Not a whisper. We're having to feed her through a tube.'

Joanna would hate that. So undignified having a tube in your nose. Her perfectly sculptured, probably reshaped nose would object.

Joanna was sitting up in bed, wearing some of the clothes

which I had brought down for her. I began to feel sorry for
her, having that tube . . . hardly cruise gourmet food, something bland liquefied.

'Hello, Joanna,' I said. 'How are you? I've come to
tell you all about Trondheim. It's a very historic city,
goes back donkey's years. King Olav the First and lots
of coronations.'

I was no good at bedside talk. My hospital visits in
Latching had been kept to a minimum. Though adding
the times I'd been a patient in hospital spiralled my
average to pretty high. The staff ran bets on when I would
be back.

Joanna never moved, not a flutter of an eyelash betrayed
that she was aware I was there or had spoken. I could have
been reciting the Koran. It was an idea.

Dr Russell came into the room. He was drying his hands
in the air, wafting them around. This hand thing was para-
mount on board ship where any infection could spread so
quickly. We were urged to be constantly washing our hands
or using the sanitizing spray.

It was an excellent idea but it dried the skin. I had wash-
erwomen's hands already.

'You're looking better,' he said. 'The wind has whipped
some colour into your cheeks. I'm sure Mrs Carter
would feel better if we could get her out into some fresh
air.'

I suddenly saw myself wheeling Joanna around on deck
in a wheelchair for the rest of the cruise. He read my resigned
expression.

'No, no, I wasn't suggesting that. She's not well enough
for open decks. But I have a suggestion which might work
well. There were two accidents last night in that rough
weather, both broken limbs, and they need constant nursing.
We need this private room.'

'And Mrs Carter, although in deep shock, is simply staring
into space.'

'Yes, and she could be nursed quite adequately in the
comfort of her own stateroom. She could sit in an armchair
by her balcony, watching the scenery go by. There is a Thai

stewardess who has had midwife training, and she could
be transferred to care for Mrs Carter full time. Do you
agree?'

'That's a great idea,' I said. 'I'm sure we could both take
care of her. And if it would free this room for your other
patients, then of course, we must do it.'

'Thank you, Jordan,' he said, his eyes warming with gratitude. 'I'll make all the necessary arrangements. One of my
nurses will visit regularly with Mrs Carter's medication and
I'll pop in as often as I can.'

It wouldn't be easy but I was ridden with guilt about
not looking after Joanna and all the money she was paying
me. I was not being paid to gaze speechless at snow-clad
mountains and magnificent scenery. My job was to look
after Joanna, nursemaid or bodyguard. I could read my
book to her.

'Now go and have your salad lunch,' said Dr Russell.
'Enjoy a few last minutes of freedom.'

I looked at his face for clues. 'How do you know what
I eat?'

'I have my sources,' he said mysteriously.

And that comment about a few last minutes of
freedom . . . maybe I had someone on my side and that was
a nice feeling. If James wasn't around, it wouldn't hurt to
have another surrogate friend. Temporary, of course.

During our entire conversation Joanna had not moved or
taken any notice of our being in the room, barely breathing.
It was uncanny. It was if she had indeed been turned to salt.

I made everything ready for her return. Nothing out of
place. An armchair by the balcony. A footstool. Fresh flowers
in a glass bowl.

They brought Joanna in a wheelchair via some back lift
from the medical centre so that the move could be made
with some privacy. Even then, a few passengers caught sight
of her white face and clucked sympathetically.

'She's getting better,' I said.

Our Thai stewardess was one of the older women on the
crew, but still not more than thirty. She had a beautiful oval

face, dark eyes and dark hair pulled severely back. She was still in her bar uniform, slim dark skirt, white shirt and striped waistcoat.

'Hello,' I said warmly, holding out my hand. 'I'm Jordan Lacey, Mrs Carter's travelling companion. What's your name?'

'Suna,' she said. 'It's a nickname, miss. Real name very long.'

'Suna. It's very pretty. You can call me Jordan.'

'Thank you, Miss Jordan,' she added shyly.

I knew we were going to get along well. This obviously made a change to waiting at a bar and the stateroom was a luxury she did not often enjoy. The king-sized bed in Joanna's stateroom had been separated and made up as two singles. Dr Russell had arranged that Suna should sleep next to her patient.

It was almost like being back in my bedsits in Latching. I put the kettle on in my cabin and made a tray of tea. I did not want Suna to think that I expected her to wait on me as well.

She was making Joanna comfortable, sitting her up in her bed, the television moved so that it was in view. The nose tube had been replaced after the short journey.

'It's *Roman Holiday* on the film channel,' said Suna. 'That is a nice film, yes?'

'Audrey Hepburn,' I said. 'Yes, very nice. Lovely film. Joanna might like it. Here's some tea. Help yourself, the way you like it.'

The Double O was still berthed alongside Trondheim and from the balcony I could see the skyline and even the white Kristiansten Fortress up on the hill. Although I might never step ashore here again, it was special. But perhaps elsewhere, there might be a few moments for myself. There was something about the Norwegian air that felt healing, fresh and clean. And everywhere was so beautiful. I loved Latching, the changing sea and the long walks, but Norway was something different.

'You have hurt your back, Miss Jordan?' said Suna.

'How did you know?' I'd said nothing to anyone.

'You are walking stiff. You must take more care. Ship very dangerous.'

I nodded. I was beginning to feel that the ship was a dangerous place. It was a sobering thought.

NINE

At Sea

The *Orpheus Odyssey* crossed the Arctic Circle before breakfast. I was on deck, expecting to see something. The captain's voice came over the tannoy system.

'I hope you all felt the slight bump as we crossed the Arctic Circle,' he said, his voice deadpan. Some passengers fell for it. Several nodded. 'As you know, the Arctic Circle is one of the five major circles of latitude that mark maps of the earth. Everything north of this circle is called the Arctic.'

He was into his stride. He enjoyed telling passengers what he thought they ought to know. I was listening. Any new knowledge is worth having.

'The summer solstice is in June and the sun will be above the horizon for at least twenty-four continuous hours. My wife will be joining us at Tromso. Meanwhile, enjoy the midnight sun. Take care. See you on deck.'

I wouldn't like to be around for the winter solstice when the sun was below the horizon for endless months.

I wanted to see the midnight sun, or at least enjoy non-stop sunlight. Suna and I had to work out a routine. She needed breaks and I needed breaks. I also needed to know what kind of straps were used to pinion Joanna to the ladder. It was so hard to find out anything on board ship. It seemed I was equally strapped to Joanna, ankle and wrist, sealing wax and all.

'Good morning, Jordan,' said Geoff Berry. 'Enjoying our first sight of the Arctic?'

'Not much to see yet,' I said. Except the endless rolling waves which I loved and could watch forever. The white-tipped waves washed past the ship's hull in a continuous murmur. 'But I did feel the slight bump.'

I let him think I was an idiot. It might be to my advantage.

'Ah yes.' He was bemused. He had not listened to the captain's tannoy announcement. 'How are you getting on with your investigations?'

'I could ask you the same,' I said. 'You're the man in charge of security. What have you discovered about this unfortunate incident? You have the resources and access to all the information.'

'Very little,' he said airily. 'Someone strapped Mrs Carter on to the starboard keel ladder. Not sure how, probably knocked her out. Some other passenger alerted us to the situation and Mrs Carter was rescued.'

'Who was the passenger?'

'That's confidential.'

So much for DI Berry's investigations. He knew nothing much at all. He'd been a lightweight in Sussex, preferring to sit in a pub with a foaming beer rather than get out on the ground. And surely it had been the forward keel ladder? How many ladders does a ship this size have?

'So what was used to secure Mrs Carter to the ladder? Something pretty sturdy, I bet.' Go on, dig, girl.

'They look like luggage straps. Someone must have been down to where we store unwanted on cruise luggage and ripped out a dozen luggage straps. They are pretty sturdy stuff. Velcro, metal buckles, double-back straps. She also had brown parcel tape across her mouth so she couldn't cry out. Can't trace it, of course.'

'Nasty taste.'

'We cut her out of it and took her down to the medical centre.'

'Do you still have the straps?'

'Oh yes. In my office.'

'And how about CCTV footage? Anything on those?'

Berry looked blank. He'd not looked at them. There were CCTV cameras everywhere on board. You could track a passenger from bar to pool and back. They had probably been tracking me for days with an eagle eye, wondering what the heck I was up to.

'In progress,' he flustered. 'Being scrutinized. Under control.'

No prizes for guessing the state of that progress. He didn't exactly have staff on board. Cruise ships are normally crime free. Maybe a little shoplifting or pilfering from a minibar. Nothing serious to report. The most a security officer had to do was to quieten down a late party before it got too rowdy.

'Could I have a look at them?' I asked. 'An extra eye might be useful. An untrained eye.'

He looked relieved. I sounded friendly and unthreatening, as if I had completely forgotten the circumstances that got me suspended. I would never forget. He didn't know I was Latching's only elephant. An Indian elephant, the kind with the long ears, and an even longer memory.

'Sure, Jordan,' he said. The man was a fool. 'Come down any time. This is my office and my mobile number.' He gave me both. Heaven only knew where his office was, somewhere down in the depths of the ship's bowels. I might never return to the dining room.

'Thank you,' I said with my most insincere smile. I could do insincere. I'd had plenty of practice in the past. 'I'd be delighted to help out. I know how busy you are in your official capacity.'

I took a fast breakfast, slices of melon, pineapple and paw-paw, then returned to our staterooms. Joanna was still staring but Suna was having difficulty with the feeding tube.

'It won't stay in,' she said faintly. 'She must not starve.'

'The nurse will be along soon. She can put the tube back in. I'll stay with her while you have a break,' I said. 'Do you have your breakfast in the crew cafeteria? OK. And you don't have to wear bar uniform here with us. Come back in your own clothes, if you like.'

She shot me a look of gratitude and escaped to the crew quarters below decks. It had been a long night. She didn't say if she had slept in the bed next to Joanna. It looked untouched. Perhaps she had sat in a chair all night.

Joanna remained the same, staring, rigid, unresponsive.

It was weird. I should have thought that by now she would have been responding to the treatment, coming round, weeping, reacting. Shock usually wore off.

I did her hair and pulled the top back into a glittering butterfly clip. She had a velvet bag full of posh hair ornaments.

'There,' I said. 'That looks nice.'

For a second, I thought she responded. There was a flash of derision. As if she thought the butterfly clip was the pits. I changed it for a plain black bow. There was no response.

'So, Joanna,' I said, sitting beside her and taking her hand in a most familiar manner. A manner she would never have allowed in normal circumstances. 'I know you went through a terrible time and none of us can ever imagine how terrible it was, but the sooner you can tell us about it, the sooner we can find out who did it.'

She did not move. Her hand was dry. I was bewildered. I didn't know what to do. Send me on a course.

The phone rang in my stateroom and I went through to answer it. It was Geoff Berry. I had to hold the receiver steady, ready to practise grovelling.

'You can come and look at the CCTV footage any time you like, Jordan,' he said, all matey. 'There's a lot of it. I won't tell you how many cameras we have on board ship. They are everywhere.'

It sounded as if I was going to be glued to a screen for several hours. It crossed my mind that I would be neatly out of the way if someone had other plans in mind. Searching for information on board was so difficult. No popping down to the library or local newspaper for microfilm. No interviews round the clock or combing the streets. I was securely tied to eleven decks and hundreds of cabins. I couldn't count the bars.

The big plus side of cruising was not having to shop or cook, not that I ever did much of either. The daily servicing of the staterooms was carried out by Ali, our invisible steward. Beds were made, bathrooms cleaned, fresh towels appeared every day like magic. My two bedsits could do with some of that treatment. I'd give him a key.

Key. I remembered that small key I had found and

wondered what it fitted. Joanna's luggage did not seem to include a jewellery case or cash box of any kind. But I could hardly search the stateroom now that Joanna had returned to take up permanent residence.

Suna returned, wearing her own clothes, a slim skirt and colourful blouse. She looked comfortable and happy. She had also brought some magazines.

'Is it all right to read?' she asked, showing me the magazines.

'Of course,' I said. I gave her the extension number of the security office. 'Give us a bell if you need me. I'll be there a while.'

'A bell?'

'A ring. Phone me.'

She laughed. 'New one. A bell.'

Getting lost on board the Double O was an everyday hazard. I had to read all the notices, check which deck I was on and in which direction I was going. I had never in my worst nightmare thought I might one day be going voluntarily to Berry's office, to actually sit in the same space, breath the same air-conditioned air. It gave me a surreal feeling. Perhaps I was dreaming.

He obviously felt the same. So he hadn't forgotten. 'I'll leave you to get on with it,' he said abruptly. 'Busy, busy.' He showed me how the replay machine worked and how to put in a new film. 'You might spot something.'

'OK. Thank you.'

He didn't say if he had spotted anything, or if he had even looked through them. He was notoriously lazy and had probably left me to do the work.

'It's all yours,' he said, escaping as swiftly as he could without running. But for one moment, he gave me a look which I could not fathom. Nor did I want to.

The office was tidy, over-tidy. Not a speck of dust anywhere, not an out-of-place paper clip, not a single piece of paper on the loose. This said one thing to me. Not much was going on in this office. Not like my FCI office behind the shop. My stomach felt a small twinge of homesickness for my shop. I'd put up the CLOSED FOR REDECORATION notice the day before I left and hoped no one would break in. Nothing to steal anyway. Only cobwebs and old books.

Nor did I have much idea what I was doing here. I was lost at sea. But that overgenerous fee was a burden and I had to earn it. So I began watching CCTV film of what everyone was doing on ship, on every deck, around that time. It was like being strangled with wet wool.

People were promenading everywhere. Either vaguely lost or talking or ignoring other passengers. I saw the same people over and over again. Did they ever stop walking or strolling? I wanted to find something that was unusual or weird or out of the ordinary, like Joanna being bundled into a lift to the depths.

It was all unremarkable, passengers behaving as you would expect them to on a cruise. But then something registered. One face began to emerge and re-emerge time and time again. But why? And around this same area? Was I seeing double? There he was again. In the shop, at a bar, in the library, on deck, by the pool, watching quoits, in the shop, at a bar, in the library, etc., etc. The man had a walking routine. He covered the same ground, sorry, deck over and over again in a regular period of time. It was incredible. But why?

He was ordinary. So ordinary that I would not have noticed him if I had not been looking. Slightly double Dutch, but it was only because I was scrutinizing every inch of film that I noticed him. He went unhindered through each crowded area because he was so ordinary. I tried to make a note of his appearance but got no further than male, about fifty, maybe thinning hair. Colour nondescript, sort of middle height, middle weight, plain features. Not a lot to go on.

He was almost invisible. It was uncanny. Maybe this was the private investigator the captain had mentioned to me? The thought popped into my head. It was one answer. Being nothing or no one was always a good disguise. I'd done it many times.

I sat back in the chair and stretched my back. It was aching, a low down sort of ache. I might not be able to stand up. That back had endured a lot of injuries in the past and last night had been one too many. Sometimes it protested.

I marked the films carefully with Tippex so that I knew where to find the invisible man if I needed to. The marks were almost invisible. Geoff Berry was not to be trusted. He'd lost more police videos than I'd had hot dinners at Maeve's Café.

I took a different turning as I came out of Berry's office. It was in the same corridor as the medical centre. I didn't like that proximity. It was too near for comfort.

As I went back to our staterooms on A Deck, Dr Max Russell was coming in the opposite direction. It was the first time I had really taken in his appearance. First time that I'd noticed that he had blue eyes, like James. Not the same piercing, ocean blue eyes, but a softer more luminous blue, reflecting some of the sky as well as the sea. I felt a wave of Bridget Jones coming over me.

'You're staring,' he said, thrown.

'Sorry,' I said. 'You reminded me of someone I used to know.'

'It happens. So how is our patient?'

'The same. Nothing has changed. I don't know what to make of it.'

We fell into step. He was not as tall as James. Heavens, did I have to compare every man to James? Dr Russell was not craggy, nor dark, nor granite-jawed, nothing like the current James Bond coming out of the sea in his swimming shorts, so why did he remind me of James? This was not the time to think about it. Snap out of it, Jordan. You're supposed to be working.

'Shock rarely has this effect for so long,' he said, outside the door. 'There are two other possible reasons. Do we know if Mrs Carter is diabetic or if she is taking medication for another illness? If, because of this keel incident, she was not able to take her regular medication, it could create a similar trauma.'

'I don't know,' I said, helplessly. 'I don't know if she was diabetic or if she was taking any medicine. I've never seen her take any pills. We did have separate staterooms. I didn't watch her all the time but I could always hear her humming.'

'Let's go in,' he said, waiting for me to put the key card into the door.

Suna was sitting beside Joanna, reading a magazine. Joanna had not moved. It was like an oriental trance. They said in Salem, in 1692, that those witches had put young girls into trances and some of the girls died. Nineteen men, women and two dogs were hanged for witchcraft. Arthur Miller wrote a play about it. A spasm of tragic judicial violence.

'It's a trance,' I said.

'What makes you say that?' said Dr Russell. He began checking Joanna's blood pressure. 'Hello, Mrs Carter. How are you feeling today? It's much nicer in your own stateroom, isn't it? A hospital room is not nearly so comfortable.'

Joanna was sitting in an armchair by her balcony, the sea rushing by, the sky a glorious expanse of sparkling sunlight. The rain had cleared and left every cloud washed and Persil white. Gulliver's floating islands. She was not looking at them. She was not looking at anything.

Suna had dressed Joanna in fresh clothes and a robe, wrapped a rug round her knees. Then she had drawn an armchair close to the balcony doors so that Joanna had a view to look at. But she remained locked into a different world.

'Sorry,' said Suna, as if it was her fault. 'Nothing today.'

'You're doing very well,' said Dr Russell. 'Don't worry. Mrs Carter will slowly recover, I'm sure. Please let me know any sign of change.'

Later I showed the doctor to the door. He turned to me, sort of hesitating, as if he didn't say this often. 'Feel like a drink in a bar, sometime this evening, when you are free?' he asked.

'This is an inappropriate conversation.' It was meant to be a joke.

'Do I take that as a yes?'

It couldn't hurt. It might help. I might find out something about the invisible man and that little key. I had a feeling they were connected but no idea why.

'That would be nice. Where shall we meet?'

'The Bridge Bar, nine o'clock.'

I found myself nodding, agreeing. But my heart was saying *please James, forgive me.* You are a million miles away in Yorkshire and you didn't reply to my last email. I email because I want to keep in touch. It's the only way when we are so far apart. So send me an answer, man.

'I only drink champagne,' I said.

'I only buy champagne,' he said.

TEN

Honningsvaag

This was the North Cape. We had arrived, after weaving various maritime courses and passing the breakwater, to our berth alongside the small port of Honningsvaag. The vast, unforgettable barren beauty loomed around us and was already creating moonscape fissures in my mind. I had never seen such grandeur, such a rugged wilderness, such uncluttered space.

'Be prepared to have your mind blown,' Max Russell had said in the Bridge Bar, the night before. 'The North Cape plateau is stunningly beautiful. It was an English explorer, Richard Chancellor, who gave it the name North Cape.'

'When was that?' I asked, already high on having time to myself.

'Fifteen fifty-three. I've just looked it up. I thought you'd ask. He was drifting along the coast trying to find a sea route to India.'

'Going the wrong way, I'd say.'

I knew the doctor's Christian name now. I had kept my fingers crossed that it was not Jack. Mirth control is not one of my strong points.

'My name's Max,' he said, ordering me an Australian Merlot red wine. 'This wine is good for your heart.'

'You said champagne.'

'Only joking.'

He was a pleasant companion, nothing more. We talked a lot about ships and cruising and people and then said a very proper goodnight. I was pining for James, wishing I could beam him down. We didn't mention Joanna once which was a relief. The doctor didn't want to talk shop.

*   *   *

The snow was six foot high either side of the road, yet the sunshine was brilliant, almost dazzling. Partly cloudy but fine – but not the temperature. I was wearing my two thermal vests, the red pashmina folded round my neck and my leather baker's boy cap, which Jack, the owner of the amusement arcade in Latching, had bought for me in a rash moment.

It was minus three in the wind. My hands were already like ice and I was lucky. I had gloves on. There was a lot of suffering going on, red noses, blue hands. No one had realized how cold it would be. Many passengers had not brought enough warm clothes.

The coach trundled over the barren landscape, negotiating hairpin bends, snow fences, plateau snow and rocks, past reindeer nibbling at moss. It was dramatic terrain. The coach stopped for a herd of reindeer ambling across the road. They have right of way and are protected by law. These reindeer were not brown Christmas card cut-outs. They were pale grey. Sometimes they were quite unseen against the rocks.

Suna had stayed with Joanna. We had both, without saying a word, almost given up on her. There was no improvement, nothing we could do, except to keep her warm and comfortable. Even Suna was bored. She brought another load of magazines to read. I'd escaped to go on a tour which Joanna had booked. I could hardly investigate the matter locked inside the four walls of our staterooms with a trance-like victim who said not a word.

There were rows of coaches parked in the yard outside the pavilion alongside the bleak landscape. No one was in a hurry to get out of the coaches.

Then it dawned on everyone that the North Cape Hall might be warmer by a hundred degrees. Passengers suddenly streamed off the coaches into the warmth of the newly built tourist centre to find panoramic 3-D films, food, shopping, loos, bars. Civilization. It was all under one roof. We didn't need to go anywhere to post a card to a friend in a letterbox that would have a North Cape post-mark. I sent two, one to Doris and one to Mavis. They would think I was freezing mad.

I went outside and walked to the furthest point of the North Cape before my courage gave in or out. The cliff was three hundred and seven metres above the Atlantic Ocean. I could hardly breathe because of the biting north-easterly wind. My throat was choked by the icy blast. My asthma was in relapse. Some reluctantly bundled backpacker took my photograph by the globe and signpost but I didn't care what he took. Nor did he. My entire body was frozen. I was going to turn into one of those embalmed corpses, not found for centuries, encased in ice.

But there were these huge sculptured wheels of peace on their rims and I had to look at them. Peace and Friendship, it said, copies of drawings made by children of the world. Call it curiosity, call it stupid but I had to look at everything. And there was a seven-foot bronze mother statue with a boy pointing seawards. Her hand was polished with touching, a bit like the holy statue in the Vatican.

There were cairns everywhere despite the notices saying Don't Build Cairns. I added a small stone. Guilt, girl, ruining the natural landscape.

I followed the stream of people down to the cinema. I was now into obey-the-signs mode. The five screens of the 250-seater panoramic cinema showed swooping scenes of wild scenery, waving brown roots, underwater swims, steep aerial drops, yellow lichen and grass waving underwater, birds. So many beautiful and wonderful, soaring birds, wing span of angels. I wanted them all to live in freedom. They had to be protected.

The guides said take any coach to go back to Honningsvaag. They all went the same way. There was only one road. I felt sorry that Joanna had missed all this barren splendour. It had been a surreal experience.

'Wonderful, ain't it?' said a man, sitting heavily into the seat next to mine. He was overweight. It was a wonder there was room to do up my seat belt.

'Yes, amazing.'

'I was expecting it to be Santa Claus land. Y'know, Father Christmas, jingle bells, and all that, reindeers and snow.'

'I think that's Lapland.'

'This is something else, ain't it?'

We talked in a funny sort of way. He and I were miles apart. I might have been sitting next to a millionaire or a lottery winner. If he was a millionaire, then I was hardly going to find out. He had no vocabulary. Perhaps he was a lottery winner thrown into the big spending circus with no guidance. Then good luck to him, poor sod.

'You'll be warm soon,' I encouraged, like a nanny. 'Back to the ship.'

'Yeah, back to the bar. D'you wanna join me?'

A jolt to swerve past some wandering reindeer saved me from answering. I pretended I hadn't heard. I gabbled on about nearly having reindeer soup on the menu.

But I loved it, every freezing moment. Don't ask me why. Latching never got as cold as this. The sea never froze over. My turbulent, foaming Sussex sea. My force six gales and mountainous waves. Sometimes I could not breathe because of the wind, then they closed the pier to the public. People could get blown off.

There was no pier here to close. I found out that their Health Service supplied light lamps and sunbeds to counter the depression of so many weeks of darkness. I was not surprised. Sometimes their only light was the gas flare burning brightly on the offshore island.

I lost my heavyweight companion as soon as the coach parked in the small town square. He lumbered out and went in search of the nearest local bar. I wanted to savour the town, too, stroll the few streets of colourful wooden houses.

There was an old lady in an embroidered black wool dress with red pleated hem, red bonnet with flaps over her ears, big fur boots. She was selling reindeer souvenirs, hats, horns, gloves, pelts hanging on the wall. Her long grey hair was thickly plaited. There was a workshop inside the house, with people sewing. Pieces of fur lay on the floor, moulting white hairs.

The few shops stayed open as long as there were cruise ships in port. They needed sales. We were a lifeline, a much needed source of income.

Everything looked really warm and I would have loved

a fur hat, but could not bear to think of wearing the animal, now that I had seen them roaming the rocky cliffs.

There was no sail away party on deck on leaving Honningsvaag. We needed lots of hot tea, maybe a toasted cheese sandwich, soup. I hurried to A Deck so that Suna could have a break.

She was in tears, her face flushed.

'I did not leave her. I did not leave her for a moment, only to go to the bathroom. But when I came back she was on the floor. I called immediately for help and we got Mrs Carter back into the armchair. I am so sorry. She's not hurt.'

'I think that's a good sign,' I said, trying to reassure her. 'She must have moved of her own accord, got up to do something. Don't feel bad about it, please. You couldn't have prevented it.'

'You are not annoyed?'

'No, of course not. You have a break now. I'll see you back in an hour's time.'

There were three short blasts on the ship's whistle which made us both jump out of our skin. They always surprised me. But it made us laugh and Suna looked more cheerful as she left with her crumpled magazines.

But they didn't make Joanna jump. Her trance-like state had cut her off completely from the world.

No changing into glad rags tonight. This was the night of the midnight sun. We would all be out on deck, playing quoits, taking photographs, still awake in unfamiliar daylight. I put out my warmest everything, ready for braving the decks. Maybe I would skip dinner. I wasn't hungry. An apple would do or some grapes from the bowl that was replenished daily.

My bare feet touched something on the carpet. I looked down. My toes were spreading over a smattering of grape pips. Not Suna, surely? She would never have dropped pips on the carpet. Too well trained as a midwife and stewardess. There was only one other person in the stateroom.

I broke off a cluster of grapes and took them over to Joanna.

'These grapes are really sweet,' I said. 'Would you like to try some?'

Sometimes I got the uncanny feeling that she would suddenly lunge at me. It was creepy. She would burst out of that trance and clutch at my throat or something equally scary. I didn't like being on my own with her any more. Yet I had to stay. All that money sitting in the bank. All those landlord problems waiting for me when I got home, flapping their black wings. Moving would be horrendous. They say moving is the third worst trauma. The physical act of packing up was quite beyond my disorganized brain. I would never find anything again.

I could always camp out in my shop. I'd slept there before. My box of costumes was there, the instant bag ladies, traffic wardens, keepers, teenagers, pensioners. That's what I needed now. It was hard for me to find out anything parading as Joanna Carter's travelling companion. People knew me too well. Geoff Berry knew me. And the nice Max Russell.

One more eccentric passenger would not go amiss. I could be unconventional, strange, odd, different. A surge of enthusiasm threatened to break the silence of the staterooms. Yes, yes, yes. I could do it. I would be someone else, someone no one would suspect as investigating the attack on Joanna.

But how could I do it, with only what was around in the stateroom? I could hardly ask Suna to lend me her trim bar outfit. As if it would fit. Nor would I want to be obliged to carry out bar work. I wanted the freedom of a passenger to roam anywhere on the ship.

Suna returned, subdued, not keen to be left with Joanna either. This arrangement was not going to work forever.

'I cannot stay more,' she said, not explaining.

'I'll be back in half an hour, I promise,' I said. 'Then we'll watch a film together.'

'OK,' she said. 'But it not nice. Like being with a corpse.'

Ouch. What about those grape pips? Was Joanna a grape-eating corpse?

I had wandered round the Olympus theatre earlier, amazed how the dancers managed on such a small stage and wondering where they did all their quick changes. The decor was elegant. Tables and armchairs flanking the stage, then rows of comfortable armchairs rising, step by step, so every passenger had a good view. But there was always rivalry for those first row seats. Evening bags at the ready, nightly, I'd been told.

So who was I going to be? The theatre was eerily empty. A steward was hovering, tray and order pad at the ready. He accepted a smile from me and withdrew to the bar, to rewipe glistening glasses.

The heavy curtains were drawn across the back of the stage, concealing where the orchestra were usually placed. I moved the curtain, very casually, and found myself in a different world. This was backstage. This was the heart of every show performed on ship.

I was not here to steal or borrow. I was here to see what they threw away or what they lost. There was a grey wig in a waste bin. Easy to see why. It was covered in some sort of greasy make-up. It needed a makeover.

In minutes I had an armful of rejects. The theatre was still empty. I slipped out and went to the nearest launderette. I threw everything into a machine, including the wig. The only item I kept out was a hat. A man's trilby which someone had trodden on, but I could bring it back to shape with some loving care and steam in the shower.

The dancers ought to thank me for clearing out the rubbish from their dressing rooms. They probably wouldn't even notice the clear-up.

So Miss Phoebe Brown was born. Her character was still fluid, in the process of being invented. But her look was on the way.

Half my wardrobe space was empty so there was no problem hiding my new outfits. Suna and I watched some late film, ate some fruit, made coffee. Suna was calmer now. But I wanted to see the midnight sun, to experience daylight all night.

Joanna seemed to be asleep. I took Miss Brown out of the wardrobe, folded her into a carrier bag and left Suna dozing on the other bed.

I only had to find an empty ladies cloakroom and emerge as Miss Brown. The wig was a bit haywire after the tumble-dry, but it would pass. Not every passenger went to the beauty salon. Miss Brown certainly didn't. This cruise was her retirement dream. I added on some cheap glasses and went out on deck.

The midnight sun was low on the horizon but it was still light. Passengers were crowding the deck, drinking, playing quoits, taking photographs. It was eerily strange. So late at night but it was still daylight. Like another world. I accepted a glass of wine from someone with a hospitable heart. He thought I was a poor old soul, on my last legs.

I was watching a riotous quoits tournament when I turned and caught sight of a grey figure that seemed familiar. It was the invisible man. He was hovering, uncertainly, an unlit cigarette between his fingers, the sun catching a glint on his Rolex watch.

ELEVEN

Hammerfest

Miss Phoebe Brown made her way tentatively on to the top deck the next day. It was windy, force four or five. She clung to the deck rails, making sure every wisp of hair was tucked under her thick headscarf and glasses firmly on her nose. Hammerfest looked no different to Honningsvaag where they had docked the day before. Same rows and rows of colourful wooden houses, same snow-capped mountains and barren landscape, probably the same pale reindeer strolling the roads.

The ship was having trouble making fast alongside the short berth. There were so few bollards to choose from. It was like fitting a size seven into a size six.

'Excuse me, ma'am, but it really isn't safe for you to be walking about the decks. You'd be better off inside.' It was a young officer, wrapped up in his waterproofs, managing to keep his flat cap on. Perhaps he used Blu-tack.

'Thank you, young man,' I said. 'Perhaps I will take your advice. It is a bit windy. May I take your arm?'

'Of course.'

'Did you by any chance see that awful accident under the keel? How could it have possibly happened to such a nice lady?'

'No idea how it happened. The emergency ladders are locked all the time, except for maintenance. All very strange.'

Miss Brown had a tired and trembly voice. I'd borrowed a walking stick for her so she looked every year of a frail seventy. I knew lots of bright and bouncy seventy-year-olds in Latching, dancing away the night at the pier pavilion, playing tournament bowls, walking the South Downs. But Miss Brown was one of the worn-out brigade.

I ought to invent a past for her, something exhausting and uncheckable.

'That's it, ma'am, better safe than sorry.' The officer politely held open one of the heavy doors for me and I tottered inside. The heat was lovely. Hammerfest was cold. Other passengers were drifting out to look at our new port of call, but returning fast. Perhaps the wind would have dropped by the time the gangways were down and the rows of coaches left the quayside.

Miss Brown could easily join one of the tours. Joanna had all the excursion tickets in a clip on the desk and I helped myself to the correct ticket before leaving the stateroom. My change of character always took place in the nearest ladies cloakroom, the superfluous Lacey clothes stowed in my capacious bag. Any reversal would only take minutes. There were cloakrooms on every deck, either end of the ship, and always near the lifts as if ascents and descents upset the equilibrium.

I changed again before going back to the stateroom, stowing Miss Brown to the back of a wardrobe. I was becoming a quick-change artiste.

'I think I'll go on one of the tours,' I told Joanna. 'See the fish drying on the A-shaped racks. They say they powder the heads to make fish soup for the Congo. So don't try fish soup in the Congo.'

She did not move. Her trance was shell-cased, encapsulated, rigid. Yet there was something that did not ring true and I was not sure what it was. Her breathing was regular, her skin colour even. The only thing that moved were her eyelashes.

'Would you like a grape?' I said, already regretting the words as I said them. Not nice. 'Here's a basket of them.' For a moment I wanted to put my arms around the woman and inject some warmth or encourage movement from her. But the emotional moment passed. My emotional moments always passed, especially if James was around.

Suna arrived back at the stateroom, with a handful of unanswered letters. 'From my mother,' she said, apologetically. 'I never know what to say. She is always hungry for news.'

'You could tell her about Joanna Carter's accident.'

'Would that be all right?'

'Your mother is many miles away, isn't she?'

Suma nodded. 'Thousands of miles.'

'Then it won't really matter if you tell her.'

After another furtive loo stop, Miss Brown left the ship to board one of the coaches. The tour was going to look at fish hotels, whatever they were, and the polar bear club. A baby reindeer was walking across the road, eating the flowers in the pots outside the shops. No one could stop him. He knew he was protected. He had that cocky look.

All at once, I didn't want to see stuffed polar bears or fish who lived in hotels before becoming someone's lunch. I'd have the ship to myself. This was my chance for a good nose round.

'Would anyone like my ticket?' I said to the waiting few.

'Yes, please.' An elderly gentleman hobbled towards me. His face was alight with pleasure. 'I was too late to get one on board. Can I pay you later? I'll give you my cabin number. Edward Hale. C Deck.'

'That's fine,' I said. 'No hurry to pay. Enjoy yourself.'

'How very kind. Are you sure you don't want to go?' He looked so pleased.

'Absolutely positive. I like my polar bears roaming in the wild.'

'So do I, really. Too late for these bears,' he grunted, climbing aboard.

I went back through security with as little fuss as possible. If they thought it was strange that I should be off and on again ten minutes later, then they could put it down to eccentricity. Miss Brown was definitely becoming more eccentric by the hour. I went up to the lido café and collected Earl Grey and a buttered croissant. Miss Brown had to eat differently to Jordan Lacey. I couldn't remember if I had had any breakfast and I needed calories. It seemed a long time ago.

The café was almost empty so I had a table to myself. A few officers had congregated at the far end, talking and laughing. I bet they had a few jokes going on. Passengers were fair game. I wondered what they would make of Miss Brown. She was going to have a penchant for being in the wrong place at the wrong time.

I hardly knew what I was looking for. To start with, I combed every deck systematically, made identifying group notes of cabin numbers, lifts, stairs. There were several curtained off areas that led to crew corridors and offices, many doors that only opened with a code. Outside I routed the gangways and flights of steps and open decks, checked short cuts. There were plenty of ways for someone to escape unseen. My map covered all the passenger areas.

A very ordinary metal service lift near the stewards' store rooms took me down to the crew quarters. Here every aspect changed. No carpets, no swish decor, no pretty lights or pictures. These were echoing corridors filled with bags of rubbish waiting to be off-loaded, equipment and supplies, cables, unwanted luggage, the mortuary. It was busy with walking stewards, crew, officers, chefs, mechanics, main-tenance, electricians, either going on duty or going off. Offices serving every area of administration led off a central block. The crew quarters, canteen, rest rooms and bar were sited at the stern.

I caught sight of Dr Russell. He was going into the mortuary. Someone had died, or was he checking the temper-ature? I didn't want him to see me. Those keen blue eyes would soon spot the lack of wrinkles and lines. There was a convenient side alley which led to the officers' mess. I dodged down till I thought it was safe to emerge.

'Do you know where the emergency ladders are kept?' I asked one of the maintenance crew. He shook his head.

'Are you lost, ma'am?' asked a senior steward, turning round.

I was lost. I had no idea how to get back into the passenger area. There were few lifts and they were the bare service lifts and busy at work. No room for an elderly lady with a stick.

'Excuse me, do you know anything about emergency ladders?' I asked.

'No, sorry. Follow me,' he said. 'I will show you the way out.'

I followed him along the corridor, passing so much activity. This was the centre of all the work that kept this ship afloat, catered for and spruce. The steward took me up some narrow metal stairs, along another corridor of offices, more stairs and then swished open some heavy curtains. Carpets. We were back to a passenger area.

'Are you all right now, ma'am? Can you find your way from here?'

'Oh yes, thank you. Thank you so much.' I noted his name badge. KARIM. I would remember his name.

I knew where I was. One of the lower decks with smaller, more compact cabins, but near the dining room and other amenities. It was back to carpets and modern pictures on the walls.

'You'll never find emergency ladders,' he said before leaving me. 'It's off limits. Crew only.'

'I was only curious.'

'Not good to be curious,' he said, disappearing behind the curtain. 'Other lady curious. She was sorry.'

What did he mean? Was it a warning or was he being polite? For a second I was quite frightened. It sounded like a threat. I needed to lean on my stick, to gather strength from a piece of wood. Other lady curious . . . did he mean Joanna?

I'd been away for over two hours. Some of the coaches would be returning soon. It was time to give Suna some time off. She'd have run out of letters to write home by now, unless she was going in for the Booker prize.

It wasn't far to walk to the next pair of lifts. They were empty. I put one foot in, then changed my mind. There was something about the empty lift that I didn't trust. It looked different but I was not sure how. The walls were mirrored, the inside light was on, but in the reflection I spotted that there was no light on the deck panel. Once the doors closed, it would be impossible to control.

Not a happy thought. Even if it was a genuine malfunction of the lift mechanism. No one likes being stranded in a lift. Poor Miss Brown might have hysterics.

I turned and took to the stairs. My asthma did not enjoy

the long trek upwards, deck after deck. I was out of breath
by the time I reached A Deck, wig askew. The door to A708
was slightly open which was unusual. Perhaps the steward
was servicing the staterooms but his cart of clean towels
and sheets was not parked outside.

I pushed the door open cautiously, expecting to see him
cleaning the bathroom or making beds. But there was no
one there. No Suna either.

There was no one there at all. No Joanna. The covers of
her bed were thrown back and the empty bed gave me a
shock. She had gone.

'Joanna?' I called. 'Where are you?'

There was no answer. I looked in the bathroom and then
in the other stateroom, the one that was mine.

'Suna?'

They had both gone. No note, no message. Both staterooms were deserted.

It was fortunate in a way because I had forgotten to put
Miss Brown in her carrier bag.

TWELVE

Hammerfest

'Excuse me, who are you? What are you doing in this stateroom?'

Miss Brown had been caught out. I was still swanning about in my brogues and headscarf. I had forgotten to change back to myself. It was a bad mistake.

'I'm looking for Suna. She said she was working here and she promised to do some sewing for me. My eyes, you know, young man. Not as good as they used to be.'

It was our steward, Ali, with a bucket of ice, renewing our daily supply. I blessed him for being so vigilant.

'Do you know where she is?' I went on.

He shook his head. 'There is no one here. Please to come back later.'

'Of course. Thank you. I'll come back later.'

I retreated with a scurry and a limp. Straight to the nearest ladies where Miss Brown went back in the bag and a crumpled Jordan Lacey emerged, shaking out her hair. I strolled back to the staterooms, remembering not to scurry or limp, and immediately phoned the medical centre.

'Can I speak to Dr Russell?' I said in Jordan Lacey voice.

'Sorry, he's with a patient.'

'Could you give him a message? It's quite urgent. Could you ask him if he has removed Mrs Carter.'

There was a pause while the receptionist wrote it down. 'Who's speaking, please?'

'Jordan Lacey. Stateroom A710.'

Then I phoned Staff Captain Duncan. He wasn't there either and I left a message on his answerphone. I didn't know what to do. I could hardly search the whole of the

ship for a woman in a trance. Though it might be worth
doing a bar crawl. That base instinct might have survived.
She hadn't had a drink for several days. I wished I had
questioned our steward but he'd disappeared too. Was
everyone disappearing? Would I suddenly find myself on
a ghost ship, bereft of passengers, roaming the deserted
decks in search of another human being?

I rushed out in a ridiculous dread and collided with
Dr Russell.

'Max,' I gulped.

He gripped my arm, none too gently. 'Hold on, Jordan.
What's the matter?'

'Joanna Carter. She's gone. Have you got her?'

'What do you mean? Have I got her? In the hospital, you
mean? No, I haven't. She's not in the medical centre. Have
you checked the bathrooms? She might have fallen.'

'Of course I've checked. They were the first places I
looked. People are always slipping in bathrooms. It's all
that wet floor. But she's nowhere. She's gone. So has
Suna.' I think I was shaking by now. How could I have
lost Joanna? I should have stayed with her every minute
of the day, never taken my eyes off her.

Max went into the bathrooms and then out on to the
balcony, peering over the rail. He strode back and rang the
bell for the steward, who arrived faster than sound. Ali's
pleasant face looked concerned, not understanding what
was going on.

'Please make some tea for Miss Lacey. She has had a
bad shock.'

'Certainly, doctor. Immediately.'

'Did you see Mrs Carter and Suna leaving the stateroom?'

'No, doctor. I see no one leave. I do see strange old lady
looking for Suna for sewing.'

'Can you describe her? Do you know her name?'

'No, sir. Very funny looking, big glasses and grey hair
and a walking stick. I never seen her before.'

Max's face was expressionless. 'Thank you. I'll look after
Miss Lacey now.'

I took the tea and sipped it. Ali remembered that I took

honey and it was sweet. But I didn't want to sit and wait
for something to happen. I wanted to be out there looking
for her.

'She m–might have fallen overboard,' I said. 'We ought
to go and look. Can't we do something?'

'I'll report it immediately to the captain and he'll alert
the crew and hotel staff. They'll be looking for her, be
assured. Occasionally we have to look for lost children or
confused grannies. Mrs Carter will be easier to spot. Have
you noticed anything strange about Mrs Carter today or the
staterooms, anything unusual?'

'I think she may have been eating grapes.'

He raised his eyebrows. 'Interesting. Do you mind if I
have a look round?'

'No, of course not.'

I hoped he wouldn't look in the back of my wardrobe
and find Miss Brown in a bag. He was far too quick on the
uptake for my liking.

But he was back before I could get too worried. He had
some medication, packets of prescription tablets in his hand.
'Did you know she was taking these?'

'No, I've never seen them before. What are they? What
are they for?'

'They are for a certain kind of mental disorder. Perfectly
controllable if you take the medication regularly.
Schizophrenia. But if the drugs are withheld from a patient,
they can go into a trance-like state.'

I tried to take this in. I knew little about mental illnesses, a
bit about depression. It was alarming news, hardly believ-
able. 'Good heavens, the trance . . . then it could have been
because of that, not shock or what we thought.'

'Exactly. Remember I asked you if she took any
medication.'

'But I didn't know. I'm hardly her nanny.'

'Surely you knew? You are her friend.'

'Not that friendly.' I almost snapped the answer. It sounded
as if he was accusing me of something. He was looking at
me distantly. The pleasant look had vanished, wiped off his
face.

'I'll phone Captain Armitage.' He switched on his mobile and went into the other stateroom to speak to him. I tried not to listen. He might be saying something about my incompetence.

'Sorry,' I said quickly. 'I didn't mean to sound like that. Joanna Carter employs me, that's all. She employed me to travel with her. She was afraid for her life. She thought someone was trying to kill her so I'm on this cruise as her bodyguard. Great job I'm making of it, too. She'll probably sack me. If we ever find her.'

'Why didn't you tell me this?'

'It was nothing to do with the attack on her.'

'It was everything to do with the attack on her,' he said, glaring at me. 'You should have told me.'

'I was more concerned with Joanna.'

'You didn't trust me,' he said.

'I couldn't trust anyone.' My tea was getting cold. I was feeling as cold. Max didn't trust me. I had lost my only friend. It was devastating. Somehow I gathered together my pride and my strength. I would have to go it alone.

'If you'll excuse me, I have to start looking for Joanna. It's all that's left of my job. And we ought to find Suna. She might be able to tell us something.'

'I'll come with you. It's my job too. She's my patient. Let's go.'

Suna was in the crew quarters, off duty from her day shift serving in the Bridge Bar. She was a slim, dark-haired young woman from the Philippines, hair pulled back into a glossy pleat, her skin as fresh as an eighteen-year-old. She was nothing like the older woman who had been taking care of Joanna Carter.

'Sorry, but you are not the right Suna,' I said.

'Yes, I am Suna,' she said with quiet dignity.

'Is there another Suna on board?'

'I am the only Suna.'

'But it's an older stewardess called Suna who has been staying overnight with my friend, a passenger called Mrs

Carter who has not been well. She brought magazines to read and letters to answer from her mother.'

'I am sorry but I know nothing about this other Suna. There is only one Suna on board. You must be mistaken.'

We could have got the name wrong, but I didn't think so. I'm particular about names. I had written it down in my notebook. I scrolled back the pages. Yes, there it was: SUNA, the date and the time she first came to help out. Nothing but meticulous.

'So now Suna has disappeared,' said Max, thawing a few degrees. 'Or she never existed at all.'

'Do you believe me now, that something odd is going on? It has to be kept under wraps. I met an officer who said that emergency ladders are always kept locked, so how did Joanna get strapped to one? There could be a vicious killer on board. We don't want a mass panic among the passengers.'

'I couldn't cope with a mass panic,' he said dryly.

'Who organized for Suna to stay with Mrs Carter?'

'It was the security officer Geoff Berry. He volunteered to find someone.'

'So he found someone who doesn't exist.' I couldn't keep a certain disdain out of my voice. 'Typical.'

Being on the Double O was so different to conducting an investigation in Latching and the surrounding towns. There I knew what to do, where to go for information, my next step planned. I had no DI James here for support and advice, nor his irritating put-downs. Nor did I have my circle of grapevine friends, who often came up with a glimmer of a hint that made everything fall into place.

This was a big ship on an even bigger stretch of water. I felt as if I was cycling on the wall of death, bouncing off the walls, getting nowhere. The good doctor was annoyed with me for some reason. I'd stepped on a tender corn, without thinking. Ouch.

'I must get back to surgery,' he said. 'I'll have to leave you to it. Sorry, if I was a bit short with you earlier.'

'I thought I'd upset you.' The words came out automatically. 'I wondered what I had said or done.'

'No, it wasn't you,' he said, turning on his heel and going back to the medical centre. 'It was someone else. I'll catch up with you later.'

I went straight to the computer room and emailed James. He was the only one left I could rely on.

> *Dear James, can u come immediately? Our next port is Tromso. I need yr help. Joanna Carter has disappeared. Suna does not exist. Pls send advice & self in person. I am desperate. Love & 1 kiss, no time 4 any more. Jordan.*

I clicked on send and hoped he wasn't in the middle of a case that needed all his brain power and resources. It would be my luck if he didn't have time to look at his emails. He often let them pile up.

There was no way I could sit and wait. Terminals were in demand and passengers came and went all day. Probably checking the stock market and the FT share index. I reluctantly logged off but would return after a reasonable time, say an hour, hoping for an answer. In the meantime, I'd lost track of time. I didn't know if I should be eating or at some event, wearing some other clothes. The dress code was pretty strict. First sitters were wandering about in glad rags which gave me a clue. It was a formal night. I should go and change. Miss Brown didn't have anything formal. Poor old thing. It was an early night for her.

The stateroom was strangely quiet without Joanna or Suna. I put on the television and twiddled about, trying to find some music. But all I could find was a replay of an old episode of *Dad's Army*. It was noise of a sort.

I hung over the balcony rail with a glass of Joanna's brandy in my hand. I felt I needed it. The flare of the distant oil refinery lit up the sky. It was apparently the only light they got in the dark winter months. I'd got the hang of how they managed to get the ship moving again. They let go the lines and then the forward thrusters moved the ship off the berth. They were swinging the bow to starboard, through the wind, before heading for the breakwaters.

The ship's whistle gave me the usual jolt. I never expected it. They were saluting the small town of Hammerfest as if it were a huge metropolis. A few people waved from the quay. Quite soon we were in open sea.

I was very late for first sitting dinner. I apologized all round but everyone seemed happy to see me. It had taken me ages to decide what to wear, considering that I had somehow mislaid my boss and therefore should dress down. My black trousers and a sparkly silver top, chosen by Doris, were as near as I could get to formal tonight. The sparkly top cost a fiver at a charity shop but looked as good as any of the posh outfits around.

I half expected to find Joanna already at the table, fully recovered and done up to the nines, ordering an expensive wine, but her chair was empty.

'We're so glad to have you back, Jordan,' said Mrs Birley, expansive in brocade. 'The table has been quiet without you and Mrs Carter to cheer us all up. How is the poor lady? We heard she is very unwell.'

'She's recovering from her ordeal,' I said. What else could I say? That I'd lost her? 'Well, how are you all? Tell me about your day in Hammerfest. Did you know it's the most northerly town in the world? I didn't go on any trips.'

They began to tell me, all at the same time, about the ancient stuffed polar bear society, the triangular church, the fish hotels and the German cemetery in the town, which was the only place not burnt down when the retreating occupation troops adopted a scorched earth policy.

'It's still going to be light tonight,' said Craig Quentin, filling my wine glass from his bottle of Merlot without asking. I sent him a smile of thanks. I was mellowing towards the awful man. 'Why don't you join the midnight quoits tournament on the lido deck?'

'That sounds fun,' I said. 'I need some fun.'

'We could make up a team, dearie,' said Natasha. 'Challenge the crew.'

She was wearing another of her outrageous dresses, a sort of conglomeration of purple and silver stripes, with a feathered corsage that threatened her soup every time she bent forward. 'We must give our team a name. Something terrifically spunky.'

'The Sputniks?' suggested Ron Birley. This was quite unexpected, coming from him. I'd gathered he was something to do with insurance in the city.

'I'll make us some badges to wear,' said Mrs Birley who had been going to the craft classes. 'I've got some canvas and felt left over.'

We all agreed that this was a terrific name. Ron Birley glowed in the appreciation. I was beginning to like my table mates. Ron had probably been on deck all day in dark glasses, practising for the tournament.

'So let's drink to the last wilderness and the Sputniks,' I said, raising my glass.

'To the last wilderness!' they chorused.

I skipped a couple of courses and settled for grilled sea bass and all the bits and pieces they threw in with it. I always enjoyed sea bass at Maeve's Café when one of her fisherman friends had a good catch. Craig's wine on top of the neat brandy was relaxing me. Afterwards I fell for the sticky toffee pudding and Chantilly sauce. It was pure decadence.

'I like to see a woman who is a hearty eater,' said Craig.

'Lunch passed me by,' I said.

I didn't want to dilute the wine so I left the table before the coffee stage. The Internet study was empty and I logged on to a computer quickly.

There was one email waiting for me. A reply from James. I was almost trembling when I opened it up. Getting a reply was joy enough. It began with my name. He never said dear or darling, not even hello.

Jordan. Go back to the beginning. Sieve through every detail of your first mtg. What Mrs C said, did, let out

by mistake. There may be a clue. Cannot join you.
Heavy caseload. But not too busy to look Mrs C up
on certain confidential data base. She once worked in
a bank and was convicted of fraud. Sentenced to two
years' imprisonment. Paroled after nine months. You
owe me one. James.

THIRTEEN

At Sea

So Joanna had been sentenced to two years in prison for fraud. Not quite so naive and lily-white then. How had she managed to get her hair done inside? It must have been purgatory. And her nails. All that laundry work could cause nail havoc.

I decided instantly that the best way to use this information was to keep quiet about it. And when we found her, as I now felt sure we would, to act as if we knew nothing about her past.

After all, she might be a reformed character. Prison might have worked its reformatory finger. I ought to have checked that cheque.

Hamish had come back to me with a fast message. All the crew and hotel staff had been alerted and were on the lookout for Joanna. He was at a loss to explain the other Suna.

'There must have been a mix-up in the names,' he said. 'Some of the girls have very similar names.'

'Probably,' I agreed. But I was not convinced. The young Suna had been quite adamant that there was not another on board with the same name.

I spent the next hour looking at the CCTV film records from the camera that was trained on A Deck, hoping to see Joanna and Suna leaving the staterooms, one furtive and heading for the nearest bar. But there was nothing. It was unbelievable. How could they have both disappeared? It wasn't possible for two women to walk through walls, especially the one that was in a trance.

An hour later and it was out of my glad rags and into two vests, woollen shirt, fleece and anorak for the passengers versus crew quoits tournament on deck. It would take my mind off things. The cold might sharpen my brain.

And it was cold. Three degrees below freezing, north-easterly wind, with an uncomfortable swell, but in full daylight. The sun was low in the sky but it was still shining. I wanted to go to bed but my body refused to accept the time. My body said look the sun is shining. It was full of energy and raring to go.

The two months of darkness from late November to late January must be horrendous. No wonder many Norwegians succumbed to depression.

Sputniks team assembled on the quoits deck, hardly recognizable in mufflers and gloves and hats down to the nose. We were issued with our badges to wear. No other team had badges. Natasha was wearing a fluffy white coat and resembled an upright polar bear.

'We're going to win,' she announced to the other teams in a ringing voice. 'Win, Win, Win.' We all joined in the chant. 'Win, Win, Win.' It was called demoralizing the competition.

It should have demoralized the other teams but they were all fuelled up on other substances and started their own chants. Lots of seagulls flew away.

It was a hilarious tournament. Few of us knew the rules. I didn't know any of the rules. I threw the quoits when I was told to throw, and aimed for the white one in the middle. Members of the entertainments staff were trying to keep it all on the straight and steady but it was impossible. New rules were frequently invented.

The average life of a quoit was an hour and a half before it went overboard.

Late arrivals were a team from the girl show dancers, now wearing more clothes but still looking glamorous in fake fur and big earrings and enough eyelashes to keep them warm. Of course the men gravitated to their team. We lost both Craig and Ron in minutes.

James would have loved it, once he thawed. He would have enjoyed clowning around, forgetting he was a policeman, hugging me to keep me warm. I wanted his arms round me. There was no one to hug me. I got colder and colder.

A great cheer went up as the dancers were proclaimed the winners. Not surprising since their team had swollen in numbers. But the crew were bringing round hot drinks and no one really cared who won.

I looked at my watch. It was twenty past one. Ridiculous and it was still daylight. It was time I was in bed, dreaming of James.

'Wasn't that fun?' It was Craig, done up to the chin in a bulky padded anorak and wearing a flat cap. He looked rather more normal than the fancy gear he wore at dinner.

'I saw you having lots of fun with the younger generation.'

'Never miss a chance,' he grinned. 'Fancy a nightcap?'

I shook my head. 'Sorry, I really think it's been a long day. And I'm so cold. My hands are going to drop off any minute.'

'I won't offer to warm you up. Another time?'

'Yes, another time,' I said with some degree of fake enthusiasm. Natasha had already retired below with her woolly coat, and Ron and Flo Birley were saying their round of goodnights. My warm duvet in A710 was singing to me like a siren song. I turned to leave.

'Goodnight, Jordan.'

'Goodnight, Craig.'

I was so numbed with cold that for a moment I wasn't sure whether I had to go up a deck or down a deck. My brain had frozen. There must be a useful deck sign which would tell me where I was.

But there was some disturbance going on from the quoits area. Passengers were crowding to the stern, leaning over the rails, and there was a lot of shouting. Surely not a man overboard? No one would last minutes in this temperature of water. I found myself squashed between two people craning over the rails.

'There she is, down there. Look, down there. Can't you see her?'

I could only see something white being tossed about in the frothy wake of the ship. It was only the vaguest shape.

Slices of silver dappled the waves. A red rescue dingy was being lowered from a lower deck, crewed by seamen in orange lifejackets. The outboard motor burst into life and the dingy went straight towards the white shape which was rapidly being carried away, but already it seemed to have stopped moving and was only something white floating on the top of waves.

A gasp went up from the crowd as the white bundle was pulled aboard the dingy, arms flapping, or was it sleeves flapping? It was hard to tell. Although the sun was still shining, there were long shadows caused by the sides of the ship.

The dingy returned to the mother ship and was winched back on deck. The sound screeched in my ears. I saw Dr Russell hurrying on deck as the seamen reported their find. Suddenly I knew what the white mass was. It was a bathrobe, the kind that the posh staterooms provided for their passengers. Not all the cabins got them. Joanna had one and so did I. She had been wearing it that morning. She had been wearing it the last time I saw her.

There were dark stains on the bathrobe. In the midnight sun they were suddenly crimson, spreading like wine, creeping down the front. The bathrobe was empty. There was no Joanna. I ran to the rails again, my heart pounding, and looked down into churning froth. There was no one there.

'She must be down there,' I shouted. 'Someone find her. Please . . . a lifebelt.'

I started to struggle out of my anorak. I was a good swimmer and I'd find her. There were lifebelts at intervals along the rail. It would be easy to take one with me. I thought I saw a hand struggling to reach the surface.

I felt something holding me back as I tried to climb over the rail. Then an arm went round my waist. It was a firm, masculine grip. There was no chance I could escape from it.

'Don't be daft, Jordan. You wouldn't last five minutes in that water.'

It was Craig Quentin holding on to me, pulling me back. He looked different, not quite so superficial and pompous.

He'd shed the smooth cravat and whisky glass image. Then I knew. I recognized the look of a professional.

'You're the retired police officer?' I gasped.

He nodded but lowered his voice. 'Detective Chief Inspector Quentin,' he said. 'Early retirement due to injury. Don't ask nature of injury. Very personal but it doesn't stop my brain from working.'

'Thank goodness it's you but you know we've got to get Joanna out of the water.'

'It's probably far too late.'

'It must be her.'

'How do we know?'

'Is your name really Craig?'

'Yes, Craig is my middle name. My mother's maiden name. My full name if you really have to know is William Craig Quentin, which gives me the unfortunate set of initials, W.C.Q. So during my entire school life I was known as queuing for the loo.'

'Oh dear, not much fun,' I said, with a slight shiver of sympathy and trying not to laugh, both at the same time.

'So I changed my first name to Bill. You can call me Bill.'

Suddenly I liked him. Not the way I like James, of course. But Bill Quentin was of the same ilk. He was trustworthy, funny, a streetwise detective.

'Bill.' I let the name sink in. 'I need your help. You know that. We need your help, Joanna and me.'

'I know you do.'

'What can we do about Joanna?'

'If she was in that bathrobe, then she is beyond our help now. But I don't think she was. I think it was thrown over-board to distract out attention. A decoy. Now, how about that nightcap?'

'Thank you,' I said unsteadily. 'But as I said, I am very tired.'

'Ten minutes, I promise, that's all. We need to swap a few facts, then I'll see you safely back to your cabin, sorry – stateroom.'

I believed him. He took me to the Bridge Bar, both

shedding outer clothes as we walked. This bar was his
favourite haunt. Some old Sinatra tape was playing.

'I suffer from insomnia,' he said, as if that explained
everything. 'I can't sleep for more than three or four hours
at night. Don't ask me why.'

Although he was still wearing a blazer and crumpled
shirt, Bill looked different. He had his policeman's face on
and it was one that I had to trust. He ordered me a brandy
(had he been in touch with James?) and ginger ale. It fired
through my veins, instantly warming me. I needed a friend.
The good doctor had deserted me, for reasons of his own.

I told him everything that I could remember about Joanna
Carter and her employment of me, except that I still didn't
want to say for how much. I did add that I was being ejected
from my bedsits in Latching and needed the money for a
deposit on a new home. That was enough. He asked me a
lot about First Class Investigations, variety of cases, my
rate of solving cases and seemed impressed.

'You are obviously a good detective but you have your
moments.'

'My lapses.'

'Apart from your lapses, what have you discovered on
board?'

I went into great detail, the key, the pills, the grape seeds.
The odd feeling that I had going into the stateroom. Those
times that I thought someone else had been in there.
Suddenly I knew why that was.

'Sometimes it smells as if someone has been smoking.
Joanna doesn't smoke. Ali wouldn't dare. And Suna doesn't
seem to exist. I don't smoke. Gave it up when I was eleven.
I was caught smoking at a bus stop in my school uniform.'

'So you think you've smelt cigarette smoke? And you
have been through all the CCTV films?'

'Yes, but I am not an expert. I could have missed something. I have spotted a sort of invisible man who keeps
turning up. Do you think you could have a look? The
professional eye?'

'Sure. And this security officer, Geoff Berry. I gather you
don't think too much of him?'

I stifled a groan. 'He is a number one prat in my estimation. He let a rapist go scot-free due to slovenly paperwork and I reported it. He got transferred but I got the push.'

Bill looked sympathetic for almost all of ten seconds. 'That is the nature of police work. Never report someone senior to yourself.'

I noticed he was drinking a coke. Perhaps he only drank whisky when he was bored and now he wasn't bored. He had a case to solve. We had a case to solve. I wasn't going to give it all over to him.

Bill was as good as his word. He escorted me back to A708 and came in with me, to make sure that both state-rooms were unoccupied. Joanna's empty bed had been made by the ever vigilant Ali, and mine had been turned down. There was a wrapped chocolate on the pillow. Just what I wanted. Sweet Dreams, it said on the silver wrapper.

'I can't smell any cigarette smoke,' he said.

'Nor can I. Perhaps Ali opened the balcony door.'

'Lock the door after me,' said Bill. 'I'll see you in the morning. This is my cabin number. Phone if you need me.'

He wrote it down on a pad beside the bed. It was C104, a couple of decks below. Not quite so posh.

'Goodnight, Bill, and thank you.' I didn't tell him that I was terrified. So much had happened. All that blood on Joanna's bathrobe.

'Goodnight, Jordan.'

It was still daylight outside so I drew all the curtains, wondering if I would ever get to sleep, wondering if Bill would go back to the Bridge Bar. I made sure both doors to the corridor were securely fastened. It was warm inside so I changed into my sleeping nightshirt, the one with the smiling teddy bear on the front. I thought it was funny when I bought it.

Then the phone rang. I thought it might be Bill, checking if I was all right.

'Hello?' I said.

'Max Russell. Sorry to ring so late, but I thought you ought to know. I've checked the blood group on the bathrobe we fished out of the sea and it's the same as Joanna Carter's. And there are two big rents in the front of the robe which could have been made by a knife or scissors.'

I'd been warm moments ago but now I went quite cold.

'What does that mean?' I asked in a small voice I didn't recognize. Jordan Lacey had shrunk.

'I think it means that she was stabbed before she was thrown into the sea.'

FOURTEEN

Tromso

I was still awake as the ship entered some stretch of sea
called an unpronounceable Fugloysundet and began the
approach to Tromso. Don't ask me how I knew. If you
do ask, then I'll say Hamish told me on one of his morning
runs.

I spent half of what was left of the night thinking about
James's email. Go back to the beginning, he'd said. The
clues were in that first interview. I tried to believe him.
What could Joanna have possibly said that would shed any
light on what had happened since?

And now she was possibly at the bottom of some deep
sea or fjord. It was an alarming thought.

Now I had two staterooms all to myself. The space was
larger than my two bedsits in Latching and I didn't have to
cook or wash up or clean. And there were two bathrooms.
I could take my choice. I was trying not to be frivolous
about the situation but I couldn't stop my scatterbrain from
gaining points.

I must have fallen into some sort of sleep eventually and
woke very late, the duvet on the floor, my nightshirt round
my waist. Almost too late for breakfast. I made some tea,
showered and scrambled into warm clothes. The snow on
the distant mountains round Tromso, called the Paris of the
North by enthusiasts, reminded me that it was still barely
above freezing. It looked a large, prosperous town. It had
a university and an institute studying the aurora borealis,
whatever that was when you are at home. Northern Lights,
for those who can't pronounce it.

It is some sort of high altitude luminosity that occurs lots
of degrees north of the equator. Bright lights in the sky

flashing about. An endless Guy Fawkes night without explosions, damp bonfires and petrified animals.

Phoebe Brown was still in the cupboard and she would have to stay there for the time being. I could hardly enlist Bill's help and deceive him at the same time and I hadn't done my homework on her character. She had to have some history. I wondered if Bill knew what Dr Russell had told me. Surely this was not a murder enquiry now?

I felt too sick to eat but I needed some food to exist. I took a tray in the lido café and put three slices of melon on a plate. Nothing else appealed to me. There were trays and trays of hot and cold food on display, fried everything and toast, rolls, croissants, Danish pastries, cheese, cold meats, yogurts, and I couldn't face any of them.

'That's not enough for a growing girl,' said Hamish, using the tongs and adding a slice of pineapple to my plate. 'Can't have you fainting on deck.'

'Have you heard?'

He nodded solemnly. 'I have. It's not good news. Sorry, Jordan, and all that. Are you very upset?' He added a yogurt to my tray like a doting dad. Strawberry flavour. I bet it had never seen a strawberry.

'In a way. I was responsible for her safety and somehow this has happened. Two dreadful accidents and one of them fatal. She'd probably sue me for negligence if she was alive. I know that sounds flippant, but that's the sort of person she was.'

'Remember that fuss at the captain's cocktail party when she lost her diamond necklace? Did she ever find it?'

'Yes, it was found in a towel bin on deck. I'd forgotten all about that. She said nothing more about her diamonds so it must be somewhere in the stateroom. Still in the safe perhaps.'

'Do you know the code she used for her safe?'

'No. She never told me. Why should she? She had no reason to. I know my code but then there's very little in my safe. Passport and some UK currency for tips.'

'I'm not sure of the protocol about opening safes belonging

to a person who has disappeared or is presumed drowned. I expect the purser has some master code which opens them all. Passengers often lose their keys.'

'Nothing is safe,' I said, not realizing it sounded a pathetic joke.

'It's too cold to sit outside. Ah, there's a couple just leaving. Let's grab their table.' He wove an expert path towards the couple gathering their belongings.

'I thought it was always passengers first.'

'You're a passenger aren't you? You grab it.'

Hamish had a healthy breakfast on his tray. Hot porridge, scrambled eggs, toast and marmalade and a large coffee. Very Scottish.

'Where's your home?' I asked. 'Somewhere in the Highlands?'

'Even further north. I was born in Aberdeen, took to the sea as soon as I was old enough, and have been sailing ever since. I've done it all. The Navy, merchant navy and now cruise ships.'

'You'll be a captain one day with your own ship,' I prophesied, chasing a melon slice round the plate. Melon is sweet to eat but it does not exactly have an exciting aroma. 'You'll be the youngest captain of the line.'

'I'll make sure you get invited to all my parties,' he said. 'And you'll be placed on the captain's table for dinner. My favourite guest.'

'I doubt if I'll ever come on another cruise,' I said, glumly. 'I'm a working girl. It's not my style. Oh yes, it is marvellous and fun and very luxurious, but every penny I earn will have to go on my new home.'

I told Hamish about my landlord's ultimatum and my urgent need for new accommodation, and that it was time I became a first buyer.

'Not easy in today's volatile housing market,' said Hamish, as if he knew all about it. He read the ship's newspaper, all UK and international news cut down into bite-size chunks. He didn't say if he had a home or commitments.

'I might be able to pick up a bargain,' I said hopefully.

Hamish buttered some toast and added marmalade. He pushed half a slice over to me. 'You'll need stamina when you're house-hunting,' he said. 'Eat this.'

A glimmer of appetite was returning. I ate a lot of toast and fruit at Latching. Cooking was not my scene. Salads and soups were my main meals. Everything à la carte, as long as the main ingredients were vegetarian.

'I'm not very hungry.'

'Dr Russell has a charming bedside manner but the medical centre is full at the moment. He may not have room for you.'

'I'm not ill.'

'You're not eating.' Hamish looked concerned.

'I often don't eat. It's a habit. It's me. I don't eat when I'm worried or working.'

Hamish leaned across the table and tapped my plate. For a second he sounded like James although the resemblance was minimal. 'Then stop worrying. Three slices of melon do not a meal make. Will you have supper with me tonight, after we have safely left Tromso?'

This spate of invitations was becoming a problem, first Francis, now Hamish. I hoped Bill wouldn't join the queue.

'Yes, thank you, Hamish. That would be nice. But is it allowed? An officer fraternizing with a passenger? Heaven knows what will happen today. I'm beginning to dread every day. I don't want anything more to happen.'

Hamish finished his breakfast briskly. He only had so much time. 'Of course it's allowed. We'll eat in the grill, not the dining room, and I'll reserve a table. Any problem and you phone me right away, Jordan. Understand? Right away, no hanging about.'

'OK, thank you.'

He was away with a brief nod. He had not been gone more than a minute when Bill Quentin arrived at the table, holding a tray with two coffees. There was no cravat today, instead he was wearing a roll-neck sweater and a fleece jerkin.

'We've a busy morning ahead, Jordan,' he said, sitting down. 'Hope you slept well?'

I shook my head. 'Hardly. I couldn't sleep. Kept dozing off and then waking up in a fright. No sweet dreams.'

'Not surprising. It's how our body deals with nightmares. We've got to track down all the passengers who came to the quoits tournament, check if they saw anything. Someone must have seen something.'

'They were all too busy cheering on their teams.'

'Not all of them. There was one couple who were rather more interested in each other. They were sheltering from the wind in the lea of a lifeboat. But they might not want to come forward. The girl was slim and tiny. I think they were both crew, not passengers. Maybe she was Thai.'

Once a policeman, always a policeman.

'I noticed she was pretty and had very beautiful hands. Those extended chalky white nails that women seem to like these days. Glad you don't have them. Can't stand the look. Nails should be pink.'

I drank the coffee he had brought me. There must be a secret league on board bent on getting food down me. The *Feed Jordan Fast* group, before she fades away. Shopping list: chewing gum. Then they might think I was busy eating.

'I might know who she is,' I said.

The Beauty Box salon was full of clients having facials, hairdos, manicures. It smelt, as before, of some light sweet floral perfume and everywhere was clean and softly lit. The girls were like butterflies in their pastel tunic and trousers, fluttering about between clients, their own appearances the perfect advertisement for constant attention.

Leila was massaging the hands of an elderly woman with a look of concentration. There was a bowl of soapy water on the table next to rows of mysterious bottles and a selection of nail varnishes. The woman was clearly enjoying the attention, eyes half closed. I could guess it was very soothing.

'Hi, Leila,' I said. 'Could I have a word with you sometime?'

She recognized me. It was amazing how the stewards and stewardesses even remembered your name when making out a receipt for drinks. They must go on a course. I wish I had the same memory tricks.

'Sure, Miss Lacey,' she said. 'In a moment. If you would kindly wait. Please take a seat.'

She smothered the aged and blue-veined hands in some thick cream and put the hands in the soapy water. There were rose petals floating on the top. 'Please relax, Mrs Katz. Let the cream soak in. It will nourish the skin. Shall I fetch you a cup of tea or coffee?'

'Coffee, please, dear. Two sugars.'

Leila went away to some secret kitchen to fetch the coffee for Mrs Katz.

'Did you stay up late last night?' I asked, making conversation.

'No, dear. I went to my bed as usual. It makes no difference to me whether it's night or day. I can always sleep,' she said. 'My grandchildren call me The Sleeper.'

'Children can be cruel.'

'At least mine talk to me.'

Leila returned with two trays each with a cup of coffee and a tiny square of flapjack. One cup was for me. Obviously word had got around. *Feed Jordan Fast* was global.

'I have only a few minutes,' said Leila. 'I expect you want to talk to me about last night. I was on deck when poor Mrs Carter fell overboard.'

Thank goodness that Leila was admitting her presence instantly. I would not ask what she was doing on deck or with whom. Cruising incubates romance. It must be the sea air.

'Yes, if you don't mind. Can you tell me what you saw? Every little detail could be important. Thank you for the coffee. It's lovely. And the flapjack.'

Leila looked down at her long white nail extensions as if churning over the images in her mind and wondering what she should say and what she should leave out. It was not easy for her when she had probably been on deck with a member of the officered crew. It might be against rules, something in her contract.

'It looked as if she was all floppy. As if she was thrown over. She did not jump or fall. It was different kind of fall.'

'Where were you, to see all this? Was your view clear?'

Leila hesitated again. She did not want to say where they were, she and her boyfriend. But I knew.

'Yes, it was very clear. I was by the rail, watching all the fun. The midnight sun and everything.' Not completely true. She was not by the rail, she was in the lea of a lifeboat, canoodling.

'Can you describe what you saw? Did Mrs Carter fall from the promenade deck where we were playing quoits?'

'Oh no, she fell from the deck above us, I think. She seemed to fall from up somewhere and fell right past. All floppy and like a doll, right past me.'

'Did you hear anything? Was she screaming or anything?'

Leila shook her head. 'No, I heard nothing. She was not calling out or crying or anything. No sound.'

'Was there anything on her hair, a band or scarf or anything? Was she wearing anything else?'

'I didn't see,' said Leila. 'I think her hair was loose. I didn't notice any other clothes.'

'Was she wearing a dark track suit?'

'No, I don't think so. Only a white bathrobe.'

'Thank you, Leila. I'll let you get back to your client now. You've been very helpful.'

'I'm glad to help,' she said. 'Mrs Carter was a very nice lady.' She hesitated, then went on. 'Does this have to be reported anywhere, please? I am worried for my friend, not for myself.'

I remembered my mental promise to Leila, a million years ago. 'No, of course not. I won't mention that you were with anyone. No one need know. Your friend won't get into trouble.'

She smiled, looking relieved, and went back to Mrs Katz, who was half asleep over the bowl of sweet smelling suds. 'Thank you.'

I hurried back to A710 to collect some extra layers. The beauty salon had been overheated and the outside decks would be chilly. I wanted to check the deck overhead, to find exactly the place where Joanna might have gone over. But I kept remembering what James had emailed, about going through our first meeting. To shift through the content to find some clue, some signpost to these unsettling events, if I could recall everything Joanna had said. I wished James was here with me. Couldn't he take some leave?

I stopped outside the door to A710. It was slightly ajar. Ali usually closed the door while he was servicing the cabins. Part of the privacy attitude so no nosey-parkers could check out what you got for your money.

But it wasn't Ali in his smart white uniform. It was a man in another uniform, pressed khaki with bits of braid and loads of pockets. It was Geoff Berry, the security officer. He looked up from an open drawer.

'Berry,' I said, icily. 'I don't remember inviting you to visit me.'

'I don't need an invitation,' he said.

'So you can walk into anyone's stateroom or cabin when you please?'

'I can. You will recall that I'm the security officer on board.'

'Does this give you the same rights as an officer serving in the police force ashore?'

'As far as I'm concerned, it does.'

I did not agree. I was incensed at the intrusion. 'Now would you kindly leave? I want to put on some warmer clothes.'

Geoff Berry stepped forward, something silvery glinting in his hand.

'Are these your scissors?' he asked.

I nodded. 'So what? Every woman has a pair of scissors, always useful. Cut a bit of this, cut a bit of that. Nails, hair, anything.'

'Or stab a bit of someone, or stab a bit of someone else?' he said nastily.

'That's not a nice thing to say.'

'Your scissors still have shreds of white cotton caught between the blades. Bits of white cotton that I reckon we are going to match to Joanna Carter's bathrobe.'

'I don't believe a word. You're making it up.'

'You wait and see, Jordan Lacey. I'm going to prove that you murdered Joanna Carter.'

FIFTEEN

Tromso

I was stunned but came back fighting. 'So what? I may have cut a loose thread off the hem of my bathrobe. That doesn't mean I stabbed Joanna. You are being quite ridiculous. Now will you kindly go. I want to change.'

'I'm taking you along with me for further questioning. I am not satisfied with your attitude, Jordan. Once a trouble-maker, always a troublemaker.'

Geoff Berry had not forgotten that I complained about his slack methods and paltry record-keeping all those years ago. His resentment had been festering in a corner of his brain and now he had the perfect opportunity for retaliation. How he must be enjoying himself.

'I have no intention of going anywhere with you.'

'Then I shall confine you to your cabin until further notice.'

'You have no right to do that. I shall demand to see the captain.' How dare he? What a nerve.

'I am going to prove that these scissors cut Joanna Carter's bathrobe in a stabbing movement and caused her death. You, Jordan Lacey, are going to find yourself on a murder charge.'

'On such flimsy evidence, I doubt it,' I said, with more confidence than I felt. 'Anyone could have used those scissors. Anyone could have planted cotton threads between the blades. You haven't got a leg to stand on. Not even two legs.'

'You'll be sorry you've spoken to me like this,' said Geoff Berry unpleasantly. 'I'm going to lock you in your stateroom until I have contacted the captain and I am requisitioning these scissors. I trust you have a long book to read.'

A nasty reference to the fact that I like reading, something which he was unable to understand, being a sports pages only man.

'Shouldn't you have worn gloves, Security Officer Berry?' I said. 'Your prints are all over those scissors.'

He didn't answer. He went out of A710, noisily locking the door from the outside. He'd forgotten about the communicating door between the two staterooms. I could easily get out of A708. He hadn't locked that one.

'You haven't given me a receipt,' I shouted through the door. I stood there fuming, counting to ten. It was not easy. I got as far as seven and a half, then gave up with a loud explosion of frustration. If I had been on the beach at Latching, I'd have started throwing pebbles, large ones, into the sea to get rid of my anger.

As soon as I had added extra layers and collected cap, gloves and scarf, I returned to the decks, going out of the other stateroom, planning to let off steam with a smart walk in the open air. My mission was to find the man I needed most. Or rather, the man I secondly needed most. How's that for grammar? Write to the *The Times* about the current education system.

I met Ali in the corridor. He was pushing his trolley, piled high with clean linen and towels.

'Ali,' I said. 'Apparently I am supposed to stay in my stateroom but I need to go and find out why Mrs Carter fell overboard. So if the security officer comes along, could you pretend that I am still in there?'

'Yes, Miss Lacey. That security officer, him too big for his shoes.'

'Exactly. Thank you.' I gave him a grade A smile and disappeared along the corridor. I knew I could rely on Ali. A little bit of innocent deception would add spice to his routine of cleaning and tidying.

Bill Quentin was waiting for me at the gangway, wrapped up to the chin and ears with scarf and woolly hat. 'What's the matter?'

'They think I stabbed Joanna.'

'That's rubbish. You were with the Sputniks. Dozens of witnesses. Do you want to go ashore for a minute? We need to check from the quayside to see if we can pinpoint the spot where Joanna fell.'

'And I need to get away from a certain vindictive retired DI,' I said. 'I've lots to tell you. I've talked to Leila, the manicurist, and made notes of what she saw. My stateroom has been searched and an article purloined. I've been confined to my stateroom indefinitely by a swollen-head security officer. Somehow I get the feeling I'm being framed.'

'Now that wouldn't surprise me in the least. This all smells of bad fish and I'm not talking about the millions of fish in the drying sheds of Norway.'

We showed our swipe cards to the sensor machines. I was relieved to find that mine had not been cancelled. That was the first thing the security officer should have done if I was to be confined aboard. Thank goodness for continued inefficiency.

Tromso was big compared to the little ports we'd visited northwards. It was the biggest city in the north and spanned both sides of the river. A huge red and black Cunard liner, their newest, was moored alongside. It made the *Orpheus Odyssey* look like a pygmy. A great modern bridge spanned the river, connecting the two sides of the town.

I could see a ski lift on the far side taking skiers up into the mountains, and a pointed white church that was new and modern. It looked like an icicle. There was snow all along the top of the range, glinting and lifting my spirits out of their current gloom.

It was a sharp, clean cold. The wind was cutting through cloth like a scythe. It was impossible to recognize anyone. Everyone was done up with every wool layer they could find. Despite the cold, seagulls were circling our ship, their beady eyes alert for titbits that might be overlooked on deck. Fat chance. They were being constantly swept and cleaned.

The coaches were lined up on the quayside. Bill and I wandered along, looking as if our sole intention was to admire the great Cunard liner. But we were scanning decks of the Double O, imagining how Joanna might have come to fall overboard.

The more I thought about it, the more I thought she was pushed. A shiver crinkled my spine.

'Yes, it is cold,' said Bill. 'We mustn't stay out here too long.'

'I'm a bit reluctant to go back on board,' I said. 'Handcuffs don't suit me, the brig and all that. I'd get claustrophobia.'

We found the deck that Joanna might have fallen from. It was right over the promenade deck where we had been playing quoits. There was a corner bit, an overhang, jutting out, giving clearance and a clear fall.

'I don't know about the cuts in her bathrobe, but I reckon she was pushed,' I said. 'She fell right over our heads and into the wake of the ship. All that turbulence and aren't there propellers down there? She didn't stand a chance, injured or uninjured. It would have pulled her down.'

'You're right. That's where she fell from. Or was pushed or thrown. It all makes sense. Have you spoken to your doctor friend?'

'He's not my doctor friend. And for some reason, he's gone remote.'

'I hear he has personal problems. It may not be anything to do with you.'

'How do you know this?'

Bill shrugged his shoulders. 'I'm a policeman.'

I had to laugh. He sounded like Mr Plod. Surely he wouldn't let Geoff Berry pin a murder charge on me? I'd been in some difficult situations before now, but none had been quite so serious.

'So how about an hour of sightseeing, Jordan? You deserve some time off.' Before I was clapped into the brig? How kind. 'I've got a ticket. I'm sure there'll be a space on the coach. People are dropping out like flies, finding the wind chill too much.'

Craig Quentin was the last person I would want for company, but Bill Quentin was a different matter. I nodded gratefully and left him to sort out a ticket. It was not too difficult. Apparently, Joanna had bought two tickets and her name was on their list so I went on the coach all bona fide and above board. Bill let me sit by the window.

'We'll change halfway,' I offered.

'Beautiful views are healing for the soul,' he said. 'I think that's a quote and you need some healing.'

''Tis distance lends enchantment to the view,' I said. 'That's a Scottish poet, Thomas Campbell.'

'Sound man.'

What did we see and what did we not see? We learned that Lapp is a bad word. They are called Sami now, people who have their own language and who have to learn Norwegian by law. This fjord was where the German ship, *Tirpitz*, went down. We were told about the Northern Lights. Lamp treatments and sunbeds on their National Health for the dark days, again. The northernmost wooden church. The arctic cathedral built in 1965 which mimics the shape of their drying sheds and icebergs.

Then we went up the ski lift which was exhilarating. The view was elemental grandeur, painted by a master. Far below were both cruise liners berthed alongside, one so big, dwarfing our smaller version. In the distance the range of snow-clad mountains glinted like frosted icing.

We watched a hang-glider take off from the summit behind us. He opened an orange sail, floating all the way down to the ground below, first nearly pitching into the sea, then swirling over the car park, landing awkwardly somewhere in a patch of shrubs.

'I didn't see the L-plates,' I said.

'Norwegian driver,' said Bill.

We were drinking coffee on an outside deck overlooking the ski lift. Bill took a photo of me with the two liners in the background. It proved I was actually there, on this Norwegian cruise. That it was not all a dream.

A thought occurred. 'Could the bathrobe have acted like a sail? Could it have slowed Joanna's pitch into the sea? No, of course not. It was only a thought.'

'Keep thinking, Jordan. Crazy thoughts are sometimes the right answer.'

The coach was taking us back to the ship, passing interesting buildings but no time to visit now. There was a schedule to keep. Soon it would be the moment of truth as

I put my cruise card against the sensor at the top of the gangway. Berry would be there with the handcuffs.

But he wasn't. Nothing happened. Bill and I strolled past, nonchalantly, taking the stairs instead of the lift to the lido. Once there, we tried not to race in. We squirted the antiseptic hand squirt and went straight to the hot counter. No salad stop today. We needed thawing out. Hot soup was the first priority. It was parsnip and orange with croutons. An unusual variation. I often threw together something vaguely similar at Latching. The skill was in the stirring.

We sat at a window table. We had not taken more than a few mouthfuls of soup when Natasha stopped by. She was in swathes of fur. Her back view was of a walking circus bear. Fake or not, she was well wrapped for the arctic. She must have brought a ton of luggage.

'I'm really sorry about your friend, Mrs Carter,' she said. 'What a tragic accident.'

'Really tragic,' I said, sneaking another spoonful of soup.

'She seemed so happy when I saw her.'

'You saw her? Are you sure?'

'Oh yes, it was earlier, before the fall happened. I couldn't stay out there playing quoits. I was frozen so I went inside. She was in one of the bars with a gentleman, smiling and having quite a good time. She had obviously recovered from her other dreadful accident.'

'Are you sure? Did you recognize the gentleman?' I could hardly believe what I was hearing. I'd left Joanna in bed, still in her trance state.

'No, not really. I only saw his back but he looked a bit familiar. There was something about him.'

'And Joanna was in the bar, in her bathrobe?'

'No, she was in some smart casual outfit, trousers and a black sequinned top, I think. Did it have black roses round the neck? No, I'm not really sure what she was wearing. But it was definitely her and it wasn't a bathrobe.'

'She went overboard in her bathrobe.'

'She must have gone back to her cabin for a quick change.'

'Yes, that must be it,' I said. My soup had gone cold.

I pushed it away and stood up. 'Will you excuse me, Mr Quentin? I've just thought of something I ought to check.'

'Of course, Miss Lacey,' he said. 'See you at dinner.'

I raced down to A Deck, shedding my outdoor clothes, hoping Berry hadn't been back to the staterooms. He hadn't. I went in the door to A708, closed it and sped through to mine, A710. My door to the corridor was still locked.

I went back into Joanna's cabin and opened her wardrobe door. She had brought a lot of clothes. I hustled through the hangers. The black sequinned top with the black roses was hanging towards the back of the wardrobe. The roses were slightly creased and lopsided on the hanger as if it had been worn. It was the top she had bought in the store on our first morning. She had several pairs of black evening trousers so there was no point in looking through them.

Surely Natasha had been mistaken? It made no sense to be in a bar, drinking with a gentleman, when you were thought to be in bed in a state of shock. But Natasha could not have described a top which she had never seen. Joanna had not worn it down to dinner.

Then I did look through the black evening trousers. There was a sachet in one of the pockets, the kind of fresh smelling hand wipe they gave you in the casino in case your hands get sweaty. I'm sure Joanna never got sweaty, but she'd picked up a sachet anyway. Anything going free.

She could have been in the casino. That was the one place I would never look for her at any time. I didn't know she liked to play the tables. Gambling is not my scene. I have enough trouble with normal money. Perhaps the man played the tables.

The phone rang in my cabin. (I am now refusing to call it a stateroom. It's a larger cabin with extras.)

'Hello,' I yawned, like I had been there all day.

'You are still there?' It was Berry.

'Reading a book as you suggested.'

'I thought you might have climbed off the balcony.'

So the man thought he had some sense of humour. It had escaped me. I could not think of a sharp reply so I said nothing.

'I have spoken with the authorities on shore, and it has been decided to charge you with the murder of Joanna Carter. So please stay where you are, until the authorities arrive at the next port. Please order any food you want from room service.'

I could feel my heart thudding. This was outrageous. I didn't believe him for one instant. What authorities? If the Norwegian authorities were taking over the investigation they would have been on board by now and taken me ashore. But was it within their jurisdiction? Joanna had fallen overboard out at sea. Open sea is somewhere else.

'If you say so.' I fell back on the answer anything phrase. 'Sir,' I added.

'Just do as I say, Jordan, and I'll see you are all right.'

I nearly threw the coffee table over the balcony. I could have trashed the place. Instead I opened the balcony door and took a deep breath of air. They were letting go the mooring lines. It was partly cloudy, the sky hidden like a shy maiden. The captain was making some announcement. Apparently we were going to take a longer route to the Lofoten Islands for safety's sake. The great Cunard liner was overtaking us without the slightest effort as if we were a laden mule trudging in her wake. Mixed metaphors but she moved on wings. Our speed increased as we left the foggy sound.

As soon as I thought everyone was either eating or drinking, I escaped again. Not exactly me, but Miss Phoebe Brown dressed in the correct code, of course, no hat. So I tied a scarf round, bandeau style. I went straight for the Internet study. It was empty.

Great because no one would believe that Miss Brown knew how to email or access Google. She had probably only just mastered touch phones.

I emailed James.

James. I am going to be charged with the murder of Joanna Carter. She fell overboard. No body has been found. What shall I do? Jordan.

There was nothing more to say. I clicked on send and then went on to Google and tried to find out about International Nautical Law. It was a minefield, or a mine sea.

I scrolled through the sites, read a lot about law and nautical authority but nothing which directly helped me.

Later I went to the late night buffet and was grateful for another bowl of soup and a smoked salmon sandwich. Where had the time gone? Overboard with Joanna? I skirted the theatre and the dance floor with their uplifting music, passed the cinema which was showing the latest Harry Potter film which I dearly wanted to see again. It was difficult to get my addicted feet to walk by. I gave in without a fight. Berry would never expect to find me in the darkness of the cinema. I settled down to a couple of hours of fantasy, taking off Miss Brown's glasses.

On deck it was quiet and windy. The slim light from the unsetting sun was comforting to a solitary passenger. I leaned over the rail, watching the waves, taking solace from the rhythm of the white horses that reared and fell. The sea was endless. It was part of me. Tonight it was part of Miss Brown.

Eventually I went back to the Internet study. A lone man was checking on his investments. *Sleepless in Seattle*, midnight sun style.

My in-mail was winking. There was one new email waiting for me. I hoped it was not a stupid advertisement. I didn't want Viagra, slimming pills or a quick loan. My love life is excellent, I think, sort of. What did they know?

The email was from James.

Jordan. I am coming. Taking some leave. See you in Norway. James.

SIXTEEN

Lofoten Islands

We were late arriving at Lofoten Islands because of taking the long way round and not the direct route. Captain's decision for navigational safety reasons and he knew best. Apparently the islands were three and a half million years old and still growing. They went back to the Stone Age, Vikings and all that jazz.

Everyone crowded on deck to see our first view of the islands. They were rugged and snow-capped. We were not surprised. The ship was anchored out at sea. The starboard anchor was let go after lunch, later than expected, and the tenders lowered to ferry passengers ashore. Ashore looked like a few huts and a couple of flags streaming in a stiff breeze. But it was sunny and fine.

'Have they got an airfield?' I asked a member of the crew.

'I doubt it,' he said, not really interested in the confused old lady beside him. Miss Phoebe Brown was done up in a long skirt, shawl, scarves and woolly hat. I wondered if the show girls had missed anything vital from their costumes rail yet. I think this outfit was from a Mary Poppins revival. 'Unless they land on a beach. They have lots of big beaches.'

How was James going to get to me? I had every confidence in his ingenuity but he was not exactly James Bond and had no MI5 resources. I had slept reasonably well, after locking A708 from the inside. No intruders welcome. Breakfast had been coffee and a banana. Back to Latching days. I was a bit worried about collecting a cruise tummy and nothing fitting when I got home.

'Thank you, young man,' I said.

'Any time, ma'am,' he said, moving away fast.

'So you have materialized today as a cross between Miss

Marple and Elizabeth the First,' said Bill, sidling up to my
rail perch.

'Does it suit me?'

'I miss the red hair.'

'It's not red, it's tawny. How did you recognize me?'

'The eyes, as always.'

'I don't think Phoebe Brown should be seen with you.'

'Exactly, I agree. Let us part our ways.'

'But keep in touch?' I was suddenly nervous.

'Of course,' Bill said. 'We've work to do.'

'And I have bars to check. You remember Natasha telling
us she saw Joanna in a bar moments before she fell. That
needs checking.'

'It sounds fishy, but yes, it needs checking. How about
dinner tonight?'

'Are you asking me or Miss Brown? Neither of them eat
very much.'

'I want to see you in that beautiful black chiffon dress
again, the fishtail one. It's formal tonight, so glad rags.'

'I don't see how I can arrive at the dining room without
shaking off the security officer. He came by this morning
and spoke to me through the locked door.'

'What did you say?'

'I said: *please let me out, please let me out* in a pathetic
little voice. He was suitably impressed and told me to stay
where I was.'

My laugh was very un-Miss Brown. Maybe she was
having a junior moment. It took ages for the tenders to get
everyone ashore. Anyone on a tour went first, their coaches
waiting to take them round a breathtaking but limited
scenario. Islands were islands, even if they had long,
untrodden beaches of near white sand. They also had tunnels.
One kilometre-long tunnel was blasted through rock so that
the school bus could take a shorter route.

Some of the passengers had not gone ashore. They had
excursion fatigue. They were happy to sit on deck and order
something hot. I got quite a few smiles although I was not
sure why. Maybe it was the flowing skirt and thick glasses.

I eventually found the bar where Joanna had spent her

last few moments. It was a side bar called Mainspring, for
no good reason. The barman was helpful. Yes, he remembered Joanna Carter. Very good-looking lady. She had been
generous in her ordering. She seemed to be having a good
time.

'She paid for drinks?'

'Yes, ma'am. Quite a few double brandies. She signed
receipts and paid for the drinks.'

That would be on record in the accounts office. Signing
for drink purchases on your cruise card was computer-
generated. It was solid evidence that she had emerged from
her shocked state and had been circulating normally.

'Do you remember what she was wearing?'

He looked blank. 'Black, I think,' he said. Good guess.

'And who was with her? Did she have some pleasant
company?'

The barman almost winked at me. It was certainly an eye
flutter. 'She seemed to like drinking on her own.'

'What time did she leave?'

He shook his head. 'Midnight perhaps? I don't really
know. It was very busy time with the midnight sun and all
the parties going on. Sorry. You are friend of Mrs Carter?'
he asked curiously, eyeing the outlandish outfit.

'Actually I am doing some research for the ship's newspaper,' I said. 'You know, a sort of roving reporter, writing
up an account of all the things that happened last night
during the midnight sun.'

It was a long story. I'm not sure that he believed me.

'And Mrs Carter falling overboard was very sad happening.'

'Very sad,' I agreed. 'Thank you for your help.'

'Any time.' I got another conspiratorial grin from the
barman. He had clocked me up as today's most eccentric
passenger. Another story for below decks in the crew bar.
I'm sure they talked about us. We were daily fuel for gossip.

The sun was brilliant. I wanted to go ashore but surely
my swipe card would have been cancelled by now. I didn't
want Berry to know that there was a way out of the cabins.
Apparently the Lofoten Islands had electricity before Oslo
or New York, way back in time. Now isn't that an amazing

fact? My magpie mind collected all sorts of useless information on its travels.

I watched the tenders returning with passengers from
their shortened excursions. The Double O still had a scheduled departure time. The tenders were being secured on
deck as they returned. It was quite a strong north-easterly
wind and some of the passengers had difficulty stepping
off the tenders on to the ship's gangway platform. There
were a lot of video owners, leaning over the rails, recording
the small dramas and near disasters. No one had to be
fished out.

I kept well out of everyone's way.

I learned that there was only one apple tree on the islands.
I was not surprised. More useless knowledge. No vandals
around with an axe.

Where was James? I knew his email by heart. He said
he was coming. And the man would if he could. Perhaps he
didn't know where the *Orpheus Odyssey* was anchored now.
It would keep moving about.

I reckoned it was a strong force six to seven and it was
blowing sideways to the ship. They were having trouble
weighing the anchor and swinging the ship round so that
she could sail away from the islands. There was a lot of
tonnage to turn. I stayed on deck, fascinated by the manoeuvres involved, none of which seemed to work. I bet there
was some frantic thinking on the bridge.

There was a long lull when nothing happened. We were
at a standstill if you could call the rocking decks as being at
a standstill. The engines were silent and the Double O simply
swung on the anchor, buffeted by the gale force. Supposing
we were marooned here and had to stay until the wind died
down?

I was missing my dinner date with Bill but I didn't worry.
He'd understand. This instant melodrama was far more
interesting than guinea fowl terrine with Cumberland sauce
and toasted pistachio brioche, whatever that was. Some poor
little bird who would much rather have been flying about
instead of being on a dish.

I took shelter in an alcove between stored and strapped

down deckchairs and some deck equipment. The wind took my breath away. A few passengers in dinner jackets had wandered back on to the deck, curious about the delay.

'The wind is too strong, gale force,' I said. 'They can't turn her around.'

They looked at me as if I was talking a foreign language.

'They ought to get a tug,' someone said, who clearly had no idea that we were miles from anywhere.

'Where from?' I muttered. 'Newcastle?'

Somehow, using both the engines and the thrusters, the ship turned into the wind, and once on a steady heading into the wind, began to negotiate the many dangerous shoals that lined the passage. The pilot was in charge. It was already almost eight o'clock but it was still light. It had taken over an hour and a half to turn the ship. A clever piece of seamanship. I hope the captain ordered extra rum.

By this time Miss Brown was chilled to the bone and went stiffly back to A708, longing for a hot shower. As I went in, I knew someone had been there. I had perfect recall of where everything should be, where I had left things. Ali might have been in and replaced the towels, but he was not likely to open drawers, disturb items on a bedside table, half close curtains.

Geoff Berry? Didn't he notice that I was not in the stateroom? My clothes had been disarranged. What had he been searching for? There was nothing around that was incriminating. I had done nothing, except carry out my job as bodyguard companion to Joanna. And I hadn't done that too well.

I put all of Miss Brown back in her carrier bag at the back of the wardrobe and stood under the shower, letting the warmth rain over me, bringing some vigour back into my limbs. The ship was moving steadily so it seemed we were safely on our way again.

I came out wrapped in the white towelling robe provided and drew back the curtains. We were passing more magnificent scenery on our way to the open sea. Along the edge of the fjord were small clusters of red-roofed houses and I wondered how they could live in such isolation. There did not seem to be any connecting roads. These days everyone had a boat and the Internet. They could email their friends or call them on their mobiles. Norway had not left technology behind.

My phone rang and I could almost tell by the shrill sound that it was the last person I wanted to talk to.

'Jordan. I'm outside and I am coming in. Don't try to rush past me.'

'As if.' I couldn't be bothered to answer the man. I tightened the belt on the robe and went to sit on the sofa. I picked up a magazine illustrating the highlights of next year's cruises.

'Ah, so you are out of the bath at last,' said Berry, striding in and slamming the door shut. He locked it. 'Ali told me you were in the bathroom. You took your time.'

'A nasty case of the runs,' I said, knowing the hot shower had left me with a flushed face. 'You know, the kind of infection that spreads round a ship like wildfire, mainly from people not washing their hands properly. I hope you brought a disinfectant spray with you when you went through all my possessions.'

'I didn't know you were ill,' he said hurriedly. 'Have you spoken to the doctor? It's very infectious.'

'I know,' I said. 'Easily passed on through contact, especially the food and drink type of contact.'

If he had helped himself to a drink or some of my fruit, he might be feeling a little worried. He cleared his throat.

'Just to let you know that you are to be confined to your cabin until we reach Bergen. We shall make different arrangements for you there. You may be flown back to Southampton under police escort.'

'On what grounds?'

'On the charge that you did maliciously and with intent push Mrs Joanna Carter overboard to her death, and that you did firstly stab her with a pair of scissors.'

'This is all rubbish,' I said hotly. 'I have witnesses that I was on deck. You have no proof. And you have no motive.'

A flash of triumph crossed his face. 'But we do have a motive. You really were very careless, Jordan. I found it straight away. I suppose you thought you would get away with it, that no one would suspect you.'

'I really don't know what you are talking about,' I said wearily.

'It was in your make-up bag.'

Now my make-up bag consists of a tube of moisturizer, black mascara, black eye liner and some very old lipsticks. I am not a make-up person. The only item I use regularly is mascara and that dries up faster than I can put the cap back on.

'Your searching of my possessions is clearly unprofessional,' I said. 'Where's your search warrant?'

'Such things are not required at sea. The law is different here.'

'So what? My make-up bag is not exactly a cavern of mystery. No stolen testers or borrowed baby wipes.'

'Don't try to be funny, Jordan. It's deposited now in the purser's safe and will be used as evidence.'

'I still don't know what you are talking about.'

The triumph flowed over him like a waterfall of vintage whisky. His eyes sharpened. 'Mrs Carter's diamond necklace. The one she thought she lost at the captain's cocktail party. The necklace you told me had been found in a towel bin on deck. A diamond necklace worth well over a hundred thousand pounds. I found it in your make-up bag, wrapped up in one of your little scarves.'

It was no use protesting that I had no idea how it got there. I didn't know anyway. I didn't know anything about Joanna's diamond necklace except that she had made a fuss about losing it at the party. She said it had been found in a towel bin and I believed her.

Security officer Berry hung about no longer, obviously worried about the dreaded scourge. As soon as he had gone, locking the door as usual, I went to the top drawer where I kept a small assortment of scarves. I often wear a black T-shirt with a neck scarf. A blue chiffon square had gone. It was one of my favourites.

I put on a track suit, anorak and tucked my hair under

my baker's boy cap and went on deck. It was cold. I needed to talk to someone, to anyone who did not think that I had murdered Joanna for a diamond necklace. Strangely, apart from Bill Quentin, I did not know anyone I could trust. The doctor was an unknown factor. I hadn't seen Hamish for days. Francis was laid low with some illness. My table companions were passing acquaintances. Who could I trust?

The cafeteria was still open but only just. It was on the point of closing. But the staff could see the desperation on my face and after the hand squirt I was escorted to the counters which had some food on them. The hot dishes had already been cleared and the shutters were down.

There was still a selection of salads. I piled on a mixed salad fast and some shreds of salmon flakes and prawns, all that was left of the fish platter. It was the leftovers. But I was used to eating leftovers. Story of my life. One of the stewards brought me a glass of house red and put it on my table.

'On the house,' he said, with a slight bow.

'On the ship,' I grinned. 'Thank you.'

They cleared up around me, putting out the signs for wet floors and beginning to mop the floors. I was the only diner left. I had the place to myself. The same steward brought me a dish of fruit salad and ice cream.

'That is all that is left,' he said. 'I'm sorry. But there will be sandwiches and pastries when the midnight buffet opens.'

'This is perfect,' I said. 'Nothing more, thank you.'

They closed the cafeteria when I had finished. It gave them time to clear everything and prepare for the midnight buffet. Feeding us was never ending. I went out on deck, refreshed by the frugal meal and the glass of wine. It was half past ten and still light. We were leaving the mountains of the fjords and heading towards the sea. I leaned over the rail and watched the pilot's launch coming alongside to take off the pilot.

It was always such a smooth operation, looking so easy. The pilot stepped across from a lower deck of the Double O on to the deck of his launch, as casually as if he was getting on a bus.

Another figure was standing on the deck of the pilot's launch, huddled in an anorak, waiting for the right moment. He was carrying a zipped travel bag. He was obviously not used to timing the right moment to step across the water.

My throat caught on a gasp. I knew that figure, even from a deck so far above. I knew the tilt of his cropped dark head. I knew the way he stood.

'James,' I breathed.

It was James.

SEVENTEEN

At Sea

James had arrived. He had found me. I knew that he would, my heart beating rapidly. The world steadied as he stepped across the watery void and came aboard the *Orpheus Odyssey*. He would help me. The man would believe what I said.

I could not go searching for him in case I bumped into Berry. I wondered if James would remember him. It was before his time at Latching CID, but he might have heard the sorry story.

I did not have long to wait on deck. He was still carrying his zipper travel bag. I knew he was there even before he touched me.

He put his arms round me and the quick hug said all I needed to know. James was not exactly Shakespeare with the sugar touch. He looked the same as always. Yorkshire air had not changed him. He was still tall, craggy, with piercing blue eyes that matched the ocean. And the dark crew cut? Did I detect a few grey hairs? I felt the roughness of his cheek. He had been travelling without shaving.

'So what have you been up to?' he asked, going straight to the point.

'I don't know where to start. I've been charged with the murder of Joanna Carter, the woman I was working for.'

'A bit careless, eh? Working as her bodyguard?'

'She believed her life was being threatened. Odd things have happened. I had no reason to think otherwise.'

'And her body?'

'It's gone. Lost at sea. She fell overboard. They say I did it, pushed her over. They say I stabbed her in the chest with my scissors. And all for a diamond necklace worth over a hundred thousand pounds. That's apparently the motive, I'm told.'

'You wouldn't know what to do with a diamond neck-lace,' he said, slamming that theory instantly.

'They know I need money for the down payment on somewhere to live,' I said. 'I don't know how they know that, but they seem to.'

'You've lost your two bedsits?' James looked genuinely sorry. He'd had many a bowl of home-made soup in the front room, sitting on the floor. No proper chairs. Sometimes it had been the only home he knew.

'One month's notice to quit. And the rent of my shop has shot up. Yes, that's why I took on this job. I need some capital for a deposit. Otherwise I'm homeless. I'll be wandering the front of Latching like Eileen with her shopping trolleys laden with black bags.'

'I'll tell them not to pick you up. How much was Mrs Carter going to pay you?'

'Fifty thousand.'

He gave out a low whistle. I knew he would. It was over-payment for two weeks' work, accommodation and food included. Mrs Carter was not in the celebrity pop star bracket.

'That sounds fishy, Jordan. Has she paid you yet?'

'I insisted on half of the fee on the spot and I banked the cheque before catching the train to Southampton. I knew it was over the top, but I couldn't work out why.'

James took off my baker's boy cap and let the tangled tawny hair run wild in the breeze. He pushed the tendrils away from my face and sighed deeply. I saw so much in his eyes but not what they said.

'Jordan, you innocent little sleuth. Push aside the sea mist and you'll see that you have been set up. It's the oldest story. Pay someone else to take the blame, to take the rap. The necklace was a plant. You have been framed.'

I knew he was right but I was not sure who was involved or how it was done. I told him the whole story of the cruise, adding the odd wide-eyed description about the grandeur of the Norwegian scenery.

'Quit the snow,' he interrupted. 'Keep to the story.'

'This keelhauling business was too bizarre for words. It's a mystery how she got there and who put her there. And why? No one in their right mind would put themselves through such a terrifying ordeal. It was no wonder her mind went into a sort of trance.'

'It certainly sounds weird. I'll see what I can find out.'

'I know I've been framed but I don't understand how. And the Norwegian country is so beautiful, it's not easy to understand something so awful happening in a place I like so much.'

'Do you like it more than Latching?' It was an observant remark for James to make. He was watching my face closely.

'I suppose not,' I said. 'I am bewitched by the magnificent scenery. I've never seen anything like it before. But the bewitchment is temporary, I know that. Latching is my home. It might even be the same sea water washing around different coasts for miles. And I miss my noisy, cheeky Sussex seagulls. The Norwegian seagulls have better manners. Yesterday one swiped the carrot cake off my plate. But he used a plate. That was the difference.'

He laughed, putting his arm round my shoulders. 'You're getting cold, Jordan. What are we going to do with you? You have to go back to your stateroom, pretend to lock yourself in while I make myself known to the captain.'

'Does he know you are aboard?'

'Yes,' James grinned. He hadn't changed. He looked so much the same. 'It's all above board. I am here legitimately, to investigate the death of Joanna Carter. It needed a few strings pulled but Geoff Berry is not regarded with much favour. He might be able to cope with a drunken fight in a bar or a domestic in a cabin, but nothing much else. The captain emailed his complete acceptance of my arrival on board.'

I was fazed with relief and amazement. It was difficult to stand upright in the gathering wind force. DI James was here officially. I had nothing to be afraid of. He knew I always told the truth, if possible. He knew I could not have pushed Joanna overboard. Good heavens, I was playing my twentieth game of quoits with the Sputniks.

'I've been given a twin-bedded cabin on C deck,' he said, knotting the scarf more securely round my neck. 'You can share with me if you like. No funny business, mind you. I need my sleep.'

'It's very tempting but I need mine, too. I haven't had much sleep lately. Awful nightmares.'

'Think about it.'

It was hard to resist but not right, not right at this moment. Berry thought I was locked in my stateroom. I'd better stay there for at least another night.

'I'll leave you to present your compliments to the captain. He doesn't know I'm a private investigator so perhaps you needn't mention that.'

'I shan't mention that we even know each other,' said James, starting to walk me towards one of the heavy doors. 'It could be thought of as bias in your favour,' he added with a touch of irony. 'A clean slate all round.'

'Not too clean, please. I'd like it to be a little muddied.'

'What are you going to do this evening? And where can I find you?'

'I'd like to go to see a film in the cinema but it might be wiser if I watched a DVD in my cabin. My cabin number is A710 and that door is locked by our ever so security conscious Geoff Berry. I can open A708 as he's forgotten they are connecting cabins.'

'How will you know it's me, if I call round?'

'A password?'

'How about Trencher's Hotel, scene of your first crime investigation?'

'You've a good memory.'

'How could I ever forget?' he said with a resigned sigh. 'That poor nun on a hook.'

'I'll wait for you and we'll watch a DVD.'

It was still daylight outside although the sun was low in the sky. The midnight sun was lasting more than a single night. It was more like three or four nights now. I was losing count. I leaned over the rail of the balcony, hugging my arms, and wondered what it would feel like to fall from that height. It was a terrifying thought. For a few seconds, I felt dizzy with vertigo. And to be swept alongside such a big ship in those churning waves. Joanna could have died of fright.

Hamish had told me that few people survived a dip in these cold waters.

It was getting late but my notes needed updating. I rifled through what I had written in the last few days. Some of my notes were wild and inconsistent. Sometimes I put all the facts on cards and shuffle them round on the floor until they make sense.

Shopping list: more cards.

But I couldn't get to the ship's shop. Out of bounds. It didn't have to be card. I could accommodate paper. Not loo paper. It was back to the illustrated brochure of next year's cruises but there were few pages that yielded any white space. I went to the desk drawers in Joanna's stateroom. She might have a notebook.

She had more than a notebook. She had a sketch book. She was not a brilliant artist but some of the pictures were recognizable. There was a tree with a noose hanging from a branch. There was a ladder with measurements scribbled in the margin. There was a head and shoulders sketch of a young woman in a T-shirt with her hair in a plait. I often plait my hair. The sketch was entitled *Bait*.

I thumbed through the pages, not knowing what to expect. She had detailed her diamond necklace, sketching the largest pendant stones with their weight and insured value. There was also a sketch of a man who I did not recognize, a vague sort of man with thin hair and pale eyes. But he was wearing an expensive Rolex watch and smoking a thin, black cigarette.

The last sketch was alarming. A woman was lashed to a rope and the rope was being passed under the keel of a ship through the water. It was called keelhauling in pirate days. A cruel and barbaric punishment if you dared not to salute an officer. I looked closely at the woman. She had her hair pulled back in a plait and the plait was floating on the water.

I shut the sketch book quickly. I didn't want to see any

more. It was a strange, unnerving collection of pictures. If anything confirmed that Joanna was unbalanced, those pictures did.

It was not easy to concentrate on a DVD even though I had chosen an old favourite, Richard Gere in *An Officer and a Gentleman*. I was only watching it for that last scene when he carries Debra Winger out of the factory where she works. But tonight I could not even concentrate on that. My mind was mulling over those sketches, wondering what on earth they meant.

There was a knock on the door of A708. I went to it. 'Yes?' I said.

'Maeve's Café. Bruno, the fisherman, who doesn't like you and the Mexican restaurant owner, Miguel, who does like you, very much.'

'That's not the right password,' I said.

'It'll do, won't it?'

James was standing in the corridor with a bottle of Australian Cuvée Rosé. 'I know all your secrets,' he said. 'Nothing is safe from me.'

'No, you don't know my secrets,' I said, ushering him inside fast and closing the door. 'You only think you do.'

I was glad to see him. He was wearing several sweaters, feeling the cold even inside. He went straight to the drinks cabinet, uncorked the bottle with a pop and poured out two glasses of the pink fizz. Surprising choice, because he was normally a beer drinker.

'From Tasmania,' he said. 'It says it has rich notes of vanilla and fudge.'

'I like rich notes,' I said, waiting to tasting it.

'Turn that film off,' he said. 'You know how it ends.'

He handed me a full bubbling glass and we raised them, ready to clink. His ocean blue eyes were focused intently on me. There was no way of telling his thoughts. He was always a mystery.

'What are we drinking to?' I asked unsteadily.

'To the first time we have met since I was posted to Yorkshire. That's good enough.'

'It certainly is.'

'I've brought along all the ship's CCTVs. I thought we could look at them together and you could identify people.'

'I've seen them all.'

'It won't hurt to look at them again. Sometimes you can miss something which becomes blatantly obvious on a second examination.' He was talking like a policeman. He was here to help me. I could hardly argue the point.

It was certainly more fun with James by my side on the sofa. We kept our voices down in case Berry was hovering outside. He might think it was a film. The rosé helped. James made notes while I talked.

'That's the captain's cocktail party. That's Ron and Flo Birley, from our table, a couple from Guildford, regular cruisers. And that's Natasha, a larger than life character. Quite a woman.'

'In more ways than one,' James murmured.

'And that's the famous necklace. So she was wearing it at the party,' I said. 'I wondered if she had been mistaken and not put it on, left it back here. But there it is, round her neck, looking a million dollars.'

'Looking a hundred thousand pounds' worth.' Even on film, the diamonds were twinkling and catching the light, like long-distance stars. 'And, good heavens, who is this willowy creature in a floaty black dress? I'd like to meet her.'

'Don't know who she is. It's chiffon with a frilly hem.'

'Like the look.'

'Perhaps you could tell her sometime.'

'Maybe I will.'

James filled my glass but not his own. We were still sitting on the sofa but not touching. He was not the cosy, hand-holding type. I'd be lucky if I got a goodnight hug. 'Who's that?' he asked.

He stopped the film and pointed to a man in the middle distance. It was the nondescript person, the grey person, a merging into the wallpaper person. He was standing on the edge of the crowd, alone.

'I don't actually know but he does keep coming into the picture, doing apparently nothing. I noticed him before when

I was looking through the film. A grey man. Yet I've never seen him on deck, or speaking to anyone or in the Delphi dining room. Here he is again. And here, look. He keeps popping up.'

I caught a flash from the watch the man was wearing. I'd seen that flash before but couldn't remember where.

'A passenger obviously. But who is he? I'll try to find out tomorrow. Someone must know. The crew and hotel staff are good with names.'

'They are wonderful, the way they remember names. And the cruise passengers change every two or three weeks. I don't know how they do it.'

'Perhaps it's because we are creatures of habit. One orange juice equals Miss Lacey. Four brandies equals Mrs Carter. The dining room waiters make a diagram of their table and put in identifying things like red hair, glasses, overweight.'

The equation leaped dramatically into my mind. One grey man equals a sketch book. I stumbled to my feet and went over to the desk drawer. Joanna's sketch book was where I had left it. No poltergeists.

I turned the pages to the sketch of the head and shoulders of a man with thinning hair and pale eyes. It was the same man. This was the grey man in the CCTV film.

'This is Joanna's sketch book.'

James was peering over my shoulder. 'So Joanna knows him. The grey man. She knows him well enough to have sketched him. That's strange.'

He began thumbing through the pages and stopped when he came to the sketch of a young woman with her hair in a thick plait.

'This is you without a doubt,' he said, tapping the page. 'I don't like the look of this at all. Jordan, I'm not leaving you tonight. You're not safe for a moment.'

EIGHTEEN

At Sea

J ames slept in Joanna's stateroom with the connecting
door open. It was near but not near enough. I wanted to
feel him by my side so I could reach out and touch him,
feel his warmth. It was a long time since I had slept with
anyone, and that had been a hormonal mistake. But this
was an improvement on our normal platonic state of affairs.
I could hear him breathing. There was time to check if he
snored.

No, he didn't.

Nice.

The rosé almost put me to sleep. And the rocking of the
ship was another lullaby. The day was going to be difficult
enough. I did not want to think about it. For the moment,
it was enough to know that James was here and I could
rely on him for support.

The Double O was suddenly a prison. A floating prison
and I couldn't get off. There was no way I could escape.
Her hull had become a steel cave, high and unclimbable.
Fear swept through me like a tidal wave, unstoppable tremors
that had me wide awake in a second. I was on an island that
was crumbling, birds swooping. I sat up in bed and cried
out.

James was beside me instantly. He had not undressed but
his shirt was unbuttoned, open to the waist.

'Jordan? Are you all right? What's the matter?'

'It was a dream, a bad dream . . . I think. I don't remember.
It was frightening. Something about birds.'

'Don't worry. Nothing is going to happen to you. I'm
here.'

His arms came round me and he buried his face in my
hair. It was the closest he had ever come to tenderness.

This was James. It was real. I was not dreaming any more. Somehow the memory of his dead wife and those two children was receding, becoming sometimes fainter, perhaps less painful. He was learning that life was still worth living, that another woman would love him.

'I'm sorry. I was feeling threatened. Nothing under my feet. It was scary.'

'It's not surprising, Jordan. You are being threatened. And I'm going to find out why.'

I think James stayed until I fell asleep. I was not sure. How could something almost perfect come from within something so awful? If the Double O had to be a prison, then I was willing to share it with him.

But he was already up, showered and dressed when I awoke. He arrived at my bedside with a cup of tea. He looked the same as always. No morning after face, except that this one needed a shave. No fisheye, but then nothing had happened.

'Sorry, no honey,' he said.

'I have to steal honey from the cafeteria. They have these little plastic packets which are the devil to open.'

'I don't want to hear about your petty pilfering. I have to go, Jordan. Don't leave the cabin. I'm going to track down this grey man, if he's still aboard. He's part of this investigation.'

'Yes, James. Of course, James. Thank you, James.'

He looked at me suspiciously. 'I don't trust you when you get that polite.'

'You remember telling me to go back to my first meeting with Joanna? Something that might be a clue? She did say something funny. She said: No one wants to get involved with the police. Now why would she say that?'

'Maybe she was hiding something.'

He left without attracting any attention so this must mean that there wasn't a guard from the crew posted outside my door. Normal procedure, I would have thought, in the circumstances.

I leaned over the balcony, clad only in the free towelling robe. I wondered if I was allowed to keep it, that is, if I was ever allowed off the ship. Probably not. They got laundered in the great laundry lurking somewhere below. Got the fancy folding treatment, sleeves in pockets, and returned to the staterooms.

We were still at sea and the waves were as familiar as those at Latching. Only they moved past a lot faster and the white horses looked racier. The pier at Latching was stationary except in a force seven when it seemed to move and creak on its centipede legs.

I had a quick shower and was in my blue track suit when there was a knock at the door of A708. It was Ali with a tray.

'Your breakfast order, Miss Lacey,' he said.

'But I didn't order any breakfast.'

'Ordered for you, on behalf of,' he said, his English getting mixed up.

'Thank you,' I said. 'Very kind.'

James, I guessed, from the choice. There was sliced melon, paw-paw and pineapple, some cheese and a Danish pecan pastry, a brown roll and a couple of packets of honey. Also a pot of hot coffee. I was hungry and demolished the lot.

The phone rang. 'Yes?' I said.

'Just checking. You're still there?' It was Berry.

'I could hardly abseil down the hull.'

'Glad you haven't lost your sense of humour.'

'How long are you keeping me here?'

'For as long as it takes.'

I was already sick of this conversation. But I dare not annoy him. He was powerful in a pathetic way and I was at his mercy. He thought I was at his mercy. He could think what he liked, Miss Brown was not under his control.

'I shall ring on the hour, every hour,' he added.

'I shall take the phone off the hook,' I said unwisely.

'If you start acting the goat, I shall get Suna, the stewardess, to come and keep an eye on you.'

It took several moments for the information to sink in. The Thai stewardess who found it difficult to write to her mother? 'Suna?' I repeated. 'I thought she didn't exist? She's disappeared.'

Geoff Berry realized his mistake instantly, cleared his throat. 'Some other woman, I mean. They all have such similar names.'

'That won't be necessary,' I assured him in honeyed tones, licking out the empty honey packet. It took all my acting skill. 'I wouldn't dream of going against your orders.'

'That's more like it, Jordan. You play it my way and we'll get along fine.'

I hadn't the slightest idea what he meant. Nor did he, I suppose. He always had a smooth tongue, saying things which had little meaning. They used to call him Cherry Berry in Latching CID which also had no meaning. Behind his back, of course. He had no sense of humour.

He switched off his mobile and I was relieved. I could only be polite to him for a limited time. About three and a half minutes.

I finished off the coffee, took the phone off the hook, and fished out the carrier bag of clothes that made up Phoebe Brown, the elderly, colourless female. She had little choice unless I raided the costume wardrobe again. There was no way I could leave A708 as Jordan. Miss Brown would have to make a hasty exit and start doing what she does best. Making a genteel nuisance of herself.

The corridor was empty. A day at sea meant a full activities programme for the passengers. They had so much to choose from. It was still too cold to sit on deck for long. A brisk walk round the promenade deck and then they went inside to a port lecture or play bridge, or simply drink coffee and talk.

Miss Brown was in much the same outfit as yesterday, plus a few extra shawls. The long Mary Poppins skirt, the woolly hat, the various scarves. And the specs. There was only my nose showing. And even that was disguised with a smudge of lipstick to give it a cold, alcoholic glow.

'Ah, Miss Brown. Out and about already, I see, braving the elements.' It was Staff Captain Hamish Duncan, as kind as always to stray passengers. I hated deceiving him because I liked him. He liked Jordan but he might not feel the same if he knew what I was doing.

'I love the sea, you know. All that movement of churning and watery waves. The ups and downs. The troughs between the waves. It's all so endlessly fascinating,' I said, in tremolo. He'd recognize my normal voice.

He seemed surprised. 'I didn't know you were so eloquent about the sea, Miss Brown,' he said. 'But take care. It's still a bit rough.'

'I'm looking for a gentleman,' I went on. 'A very grey sort of gentleman. By himself, I think. Thinning hair, sort of remote. Doesn't mix much. Always on the fringe of things. A bit like me,' I added.

'Strangely enough, I think I know who you mean,' said Hamish. 'I've noticed him at a few parties, always on the edge. But he wasn't on deck for the midnight sun fun and games. Far too sensible. Long taken to his bed.'

'Do you know who he is?'

'No, sorry. It's impossible to learn everyone's name. Only the charming ones,' he added with the slightest incline of his head. He moved on swiftly. He didn't want to be stuck with me till lunch time.

So the grey man did exist. He had been noticed. If Hamish had spotted him so maybe had others. I needed to do a bit more digging. My first round was the bars, again. Miss Brown would be getting a reputation.

I traded my customary orange juice for pineapple juice. But all this liquid consumption soon began to pay dividends. Apart from going in and out of the loos. Yes, the grey man had been noticed by the bar staff, drinking alone, rarely speaking. His favourite drink: vodka and apple juice.

It wasn't much to go on, an unusual drink. But the bar staff were brilliant. Yes, they remembered him, always on his own, drank quite a lot, unsociable. They could not remember his name or cabin number. He smoked, they said, and had to leave the bar for the smoking room.

Somehow I had to look at the bar receipts for the last few days, to look for the same name cropping up. A big order. How was I going to manage that? I needed help. A master plan. Bill Quentin.

Bill was in the cafeteria, surrounded by empty cups of

coffee and sheets of paper. He nodded towards the seat opposite, half rising. Bill was in his usual layers of sweaters and fleece. He'd never stand the Antarctic.

'Miss Brown. Charmed to see you. Like a cup of coffee? You look as if you need something.'

'Thank you, Mr Quentin. What are you doing?'

'The four skills of detecting are statements, interviews, recording, collating and I've interviewed practically everyone who was at the midnight sun quoits tournament. I've checked and rechecked statement against statement. Often a small, neglected item is the one that produces results. And these results are interesting.'

I sat down with a cup of black coffee, not waiting to hear those interesting results. I needed an adrenaline boost. 'And I've discovered that we have a mystery man aboard. A grey man who appears on the edge of photographs. Can you help me find out who he is? I've discovered he drinks only vodka and apple juice. He tours the bars at night, always alone. I need to look at the bar receipts. How can I do that? He also smokes. Can you help me?'

'Ah, I have a friend in accounts who might be persuaded to allow me to look at his computer records. I would not dream of asking if I could look at them without good reason, but if I take him into my confidence, make him an associate of sorts. He might be persuaded.'

'Terrific. Let me know as soon as you know anything. It could be important, it could be nothing.'

'I know the feeling.'

'You are much nicer than I first thought,' I said.

'It's a well kept secret,' he agreed.

At that moment there was the strangest grinding noise from nowhere. And a shudder that vibrated through the entire ship. The coffee on the table slid a few inches, then stopped. We looked out of the window and saw that the Double O was not moving. She was rocking but not moving.

'We've stopped,' said Bill. 'Let's go and find out why.'

We went up on deck, bracing the cold. A few passengers had noticed the change but the other several hundred were busy doing what passengers do best, eating, drinking and talking. We hung over the rail, staring at the waves, wondering why we were not moving. Nothing was happening down below. The waves were splashing against the hull very much like the tide moving in towards the sloped shingle on the beach at Latching.

'What's happening?' I asked a passing officer.

'Nothing to worry about, ma'am.'

Routine assurance. They did it so well. They were trained for all emergencies and I had a feeling this was an emergency. I could feel a tenseness in the air. The huge ship was at a standstill and there was nothing obvious, no refugees waving from a dingy, no luxury yacht in distress, no man overboard.

'But we are not moving,' I said.

'Probably checking the engines, ma'am,' he said, before moving on.

The tannoy came on. 'Midday watch on air. Midday watch on air. I repeat, midday watch on air.'

'That's a coded message to the crew,' said Bill Quentin, pushing me away from the rail. 'It means something entirely different. Go forward, to the front of the ship. Move, Jordan.'

We began to move against the surge of curious passengers hurrying to the rails. The grapevine had been working faster than any message from the captain. They knew something was wrong and wanted to see what it was. Videos were out and switched on, fodder for winter parties. Maybe dolphins or whales.

The decks were rocking but not level. There was a slight tilt. I could feel the difference beneath my feet. Before we reached even the furthermost deck, it was obvious that the Double O was in trouble. The great ship had gone aground. She was not moving and her deck was tilted.

'Do you know where we are?' I asked.

'Somewhere near the Vallesgrund, I think. Part of the North Sea that is notorious for sailors and ships. Near Bird Island.'

Suddenly I was nervous. Bird Island. It broke my dream. I had dreamed of an island covered in birds, not exactly like the Hitchcock film, but an island that had disintegrated beneath my feet and became a seething mass of live feathers. Fragments of the dream flooded into my head.

'Something's wrong,' I cried out. 'It's broken my dream.'

'Too right, my girl. Let's get away from here.'

'Why?'

'Don't ask why, do as I say. And don't look. Over there, by the lifeboat, on his own, is a grey man. Don't let him see you.'

NINETEEN

Aground

The *Orpheus Odyssey* was aground. It was stuck, not in any ungainly way, more like a motionless swan caught in the reeds. The rough waves were still crashing round her hull. It was stuck all those metres down on some unexpected high ridge in a shallow seabed. The ship was out at sea but nearby was an island, a craggy rocky cliff-face swarming with thousands of seabirds.

'Is that our man?' I asked as Bill turned and moved away, not hurrying. He didn't want to draw attention.

'I'd say it was. But let's hope we can find someone to identify him.'

'How?'

'Let's elicit the help of a friendly bar steward. Let's see if a vodka and apple juice tempts him.'

Bill left me looking at Bird Island. He returned, closely followed by a steward with a tray. On it was a tall glass, the ice glinting in the cloudy liquid. He went towards the distant figure standing alone. There seemed to be some conversation, then the man took the glass and signed a chit.

Bill nodded. 'It's worked. He's taken the drink and signed for it. Now we only have to see what name he's using.'

'You don't think he's using his real name?'

'I doubt it.'

'That looks like a nesting cliff,' I said, trying to assume we had nothing to do with this small incident. 'Is this a deliberate port of call? Something different, something to surprise us? One of the captain's jokes.'

'I doubt it. We are aground. Look at the activity. The crew are rushing about everywhere. All hands on deck.'

'Perhaps this is a good time to make our more sensitive enquiries, separately.'

'Atta, girl. Go to it. See you around.'

Bill was gone in a moment, merged with the passengers crowding on deck to find out why the ship was not moving. I was on my own. The island looked wild and untamed. The ship felt wild and untamed. The captain was not in control, nor the crew. The ship had done this grounding thing all on her own. She was using her own will. We were both on our own. I ran my hand along the rail, touching her, trying to reach her soul.

'We'll be all right,' I whispered to the ship. 'You and me together. Don't panic.'

The captain's voice came over the loudspeaker, clear and calm. 'This is Captain Armitage, speaking from the bridge. As you are aware, the *Orpheus Odyssey* is not moving. This is a purely temporary situation and we will be on our way as soon as possible. In the meantime, carry on enjoying yourself and leave it to the crew to get us moving again.'

There was some sort of crackle over the loudspeaker, then the captain spoke again. I could hear the birds flying to and from the island, twittering and wings flapping, a chorus of wild life, disturbed by the strange new image so close to their sanctuary, big and menacing.

'I do assure you that the *Orpheus* has not broken down. It is in perfect working order. Our engines are in tip-top condition. No navigational problems. It's a very minor hiccup and we shall soon be on our way.'

Like being aground is only a minor hiccup. There was another crackle over the loudspeaker and a different voice joined in the announcements. No sign of panic as yet.

'This is your security officer Geoff Berry speaking. This is a request for Miss Jordan Lacey to make herself known to a member of the crew. When she will hear something to her advantage. Miss Jordan Lacey. We have some good news for you. Very good news.'

There was an air of false sincerity to his speech. I didn't believe a word. He was lying through his amalgam fillings.

Somehow he had discovered that I was no longer in the stateroom and he wanted to find me, fast. Good news, my foot. Jordan Lacey was going to run aground too. I would miss the shower, the comfortable bed, the daily supply of ice and Ali's good care. No more thick white towels or sitting on the balcony. Phoebe Brown would have to wash in the ladies' loo and use paper tissues to dry off.

Miss Brown's capacious handbag held everything I might need for a short time. My notes, a toothbrush and some mascara. It was a habit to carry mascara although Phoebe did not use eye make-up, only a pale foundation to fade out the eyebrows. Tomorrow would be different, but like Scarlett O'Hara, I'd worry about that tomorrow.

Staff Captain Hamish Duncan was also hurrying along the deck going towards the bridge. I could not resist stepping in front of him. A look of resignation flashed across his face but he stopped politely. The thick glasses guarded my eyes.

'What's happening, Captain?' I asked tremulously, giving him instant promotion. 'I'm so worried.'

'Nothing to worry about, ma'am. Everything is under control. Now, if you don't mind, I've a lot to do.'

'I have every confidence in you.'

'That's very reassuring.'

Hamish was away before I could thank him. He had evasion down to a fine art. I was still deceiving him. It was unforgivable. Someday I would have to make it up to him in a roundabout sort of way, something clever and subtle. It was beyond my currently frozen imagination to think up how. James was here. He'd know what to do.

Of course, if the hull of the *Orpheus* was holed, we'd be donning life jackets any moment and herded into the lifeboats. The lifeboats were not heated. But rows of body heat would help. My life jacket was in the stateroom. There must be spares on the lifeboats.

'Where are we?' I asked, waylaying another member of the crew.

'Norskehavet.'

I'd asked the wrong person.

It was easy to spot the doctor. Max Russell was going somewhere with his medical bag, making a cabin visit. Some poor soul who didn't know whether the ship was moving or not, nor caring very much, if they were spending most of the time hung over in the bathroom.

'Dr Russell,' I said. 'No one will tell me. Has the ship been damaged? Has she been holed?'

'No, of course, not. We are quite safe. It's only a minor disruption. We shall soon be on our way and heading for Bergen. Now, if you'll excuse me, I've a cabin call to make.' He turned on his heel, ready to continue on his way.

'I've just seen Jordan Lacey, that young woman with all the sort of reddish hair, the one they are advertising for,' I said with instant inspiration. 'She asked me if I knew what was the good news waiting for her. Do you know what it is? She's dying to know.'

Max Russell stopped abruptly. 'You've seen her? Where is she? This young woman, Jordan Lacey? You've spoken to her?'

'Why, yes. I saw her only moments ago. She was jogging on the promenade deck, keeping fit, I expect. She has such a lovely figure. Wearing a pretty blue track suit and all that hair, tied back with a ribbon. She was going round and round. Quite made me giddy.'

Max Russell was on his phone immediately. He turned his back on me. Not very polite when I'd been so useful.

'Berry? She's on the promenade deck, jogging. Blue track suit.'

There was a pause and I wondered what Geoff Berry was saying. I couldn't hear a word. He was probably marshalling his forces for a full-scale invasion of the promenade deck. It would be organized on police terms, lots of plastic tape cordoning off the area. He didn't have any police dogs.

'I'll ask my informant,' said Max. He turned to me, seeing only the shapeless bundle of Miss Brown. 'Do you know what time this was, when you saw Jordan Lacey?'

'About ten minutes ago, I think, I mean . . . I don't exactly know,' I said, getting all flustered. 'Is it important? Is the young lady in trouble? She is such a nice person. Very kind and always a pleasant word.'

'Yes, yes,' he interrupted. 'But can you give me the exact time?'

'Oh dear. I'm sorry, I–I really can't remember. I'm not very good with times. So much has been happening with the ship stopping and everything. I didn't give it a thought.'

He was not looking at me which was a relief. I couldn't disguise my eyes. He might recognize them from the time when he had gazed into them with interest. Where had that nice doctor gone? He had vanished and yet I was not usually wrong about people. Something must have happened to change his attitude towards me, towards Jordan Lacey in particular. I couldn't think what I had done to earn his displeasure. One minute he was buying me a brandy with intent, and the next he couldn't bear the sight of me.

'No, she's still here.' He handed me his phone. 'The security officer wants to talk to you.'

'Oh dear, no,' I said, my hand fluttering to my throat. 'I couldn't. I wouldn't know what to say to him. He's very important, isn't he?'

From past experience in court cases, I knew that it's never a good idea to talk too much when giving evidence. It's only too easy to be tripped up by the defence counsel, easy to say too much which doesn't quite tie up with your original story or the facts.

Max handed me his phone impatiently. 'Just tell him what you've told me.'

I took the phone, then pretended to fumble it and cleverly disconnected the line. 'Hello . . . hello . . . Oh dear, I am sorry, there doesn't seem to be anyone there. I can never get the hang of these new-fangled contraptions. Now, I must just spend a penny . . .' I wandered off, leaving a furious looking Max to take back his mobile in disgust at my total incompetence.

The ladies cloakroom was empty. Everyone was on deck, not wanting to miss a moment of the drama. There was an air of apprehension among those who understood what was going on or not going on.

Bird Island looked close and the birds were still agitated, squawking in distress and flying back to their nests to protect their eggs or chicks. The time of the season was crucial but I had no idea of their nesting timetable.

I went into a cubicle, put the lid down and sat down on the seat. This was a fine state of affairs. I was on the run, had only the clothes I stood up in, no cruise card that would pay for anything. Food was less of a problem as the cafeteria was open nearly all hours. And there were water fountains around on deck. But where would I sleep? The night cleaners would soon find me if I tried to sleep on a lounge sofa.

Suddenly I was very tired. My head was beginning to ache. Only three more days and we would be back at Southampton, that is if they got her moving. I could bluff my way off the ship, lost my swipe card, left it in the cabin, etc., luggage being carried by kind porter, etc. Or perhaps I could slip off at Bergen, if we ever got there, and somehow find my way back to Latching.

I was suddenly homesick for the pier, the sea, the long walks along the beach, my noisy seagulls. All my good friends.

But meanwhile I had to keep out of sight, out of mind, while Berry searched the ship from top to bottom. He wouldn't give up till he found me now that he knew I was on the loose.

Footsteps came into the cloakroom, heels clicking on the tiled floor. A woman was humming, running water, washing her hands and then repairing her make-up. She was taking a long time about it, humming under her breath.

I kept very still. I had heard that tuneless humming many times before. Coming from the other bathroom in the stateroom as Joanna did her make-up, applying the layers, disguising the wrinkles and lines. She was an artist, painting on her face every day.

It sounded like Joanna Carter. I peered through the tiny crack by the door hinge, trying not to breathe. It was Joanna

Carter. She was alive and well and doing her face in an empty cloakroom. For a moment my head swam with confusion. She was supposed to be dead, lying at the bottom of a fjord.

And I was under arrest for her murder.

TWENTY

Still at Sea

Joanna Carter was very much alive and well. I could barely believe my eyes, trying to take in all the implications. And I was being charged with her murder. Why hadn't she come forward to clear my name? Perhaps she didn't know what had happened. Perhaps she had lost her memory. She had been in that dreadful trance state for days.

I wanted to rush out and hug her, congratulate her on her recovery, go somewhere together to celebrate my freedom. My own clothes again, a decent bed, luxury towels galore. Bliss.

But a sense of caution stopped me. Why hadn't she made her survival known to Dr Russell or Geoff Berry? They both thought she was dead, victim by my hand. I peered through the crack again. She was wearing different clothes, less elegant, quite plain and ordinary, looking unglamorous with Seventies rimmed glasses and her blonde hair tucked into a turban. She was dialling on her mobile phone.

'Ollie? She's got out. Yes, that damned fool Berry didn't lock both doors to the staterooms. Idiot. So she's swanning around the ship, probably poking her nose into everything, being a damned nuisance. But someone is bound to spot her. It can't be for long.'

Ollie? That name rang a bell but I couldn't place it. And she knew about Berry locking me into the stateroom. Did Berry know she was alive? Surely not, he was investigating her murder with all the energy he could muster.

'Yes, we're aground, dammit, but it won't be for long. And there's a mist rolling in. Can't wait to get back to Southampton and get things moving. Of course, we could

get off at Bergen and fly home. Now, that's an idea. There's
a good airport nearby. Money no object now.' She gave a
short laugh. It rang like a ship's bell with a crack.

This was more and more intriguing. She wanted to get
things moving. What things? But if she went ashore
at Bergen and disappeared into the thin Norwegian
air there would be no way of proving my innocence. I
would have to stop her. James could do this. He had the
authority.

'I'll need to get my passport out of the cabin safe,' she
went on. 'And pick up a few decent clothes. I'm sick of
these ghastly old things. Only for the Gatwick arrivals
control, you understand, then the passport can go in a bin.
I'd like a new name, something really cool and glamorous.
You can get me a new passport, can't you? You said you
could. I've always disliked Joanna. Too boyish for me. Do
you like Dolores? Or Samantha?'

I was stunned. She was going to bin her current passport, get a new name. Some things were falling into place
like a jigsaw but I was not sure what pieces they were
or the picture they made. She was going to get herself a
new identity. It was horrendously confusing and a motive
of sorts was emerging but I could not recognize what
it was.

'The diamond necklace will be a problem, but it's your
problem, Ollie darling. Berry has got it as evidence, locked
away in his little night safe. You'll have to claim it back
when we return to England. Sign a few forms. A nuisance,
I know.' She sighed deeply. 'But it's me who has done
everything so far. About time you did your bit.

'I had to give it to him. I had no choice. He was turning
nasty. It was a sort of insurance.' She laughed again at the
word. 'Don't worry. I've plenty of euros, tucked away in my
jewellery box, the one you gave me, with the special key.'

She sprayed herself liberally with Dior's Pure Poison,
still humming.

There was a pause. 'OK, so it has to be room service
again. I'm sick of room service but, as you say, the dining
room would be too dangerous. Someone would be bound

to recognize me and come rushing over to congratulate me on my miraculous recovery. For heaven's sake, don't worry about the girl. She'll probably get off lightly for good behaviour or something.'

With a clatter of heels on the tiled floor, she left the cloakroom. The ship was still not moving. I crept out of the cubicle. By the washbasin was a slender silver tube. She had left her lipstick behind. I wrapped it carefully in a tissue and put it in my bag. It might still have fingerprints. I didn't know if lipstick would carry DNA. Somehow I had to get it date stamped or someone could argue that I'd acquired it days ago. It was a slender chance.

I went straight to the photo salon where passengers ordered all the set photos, getting on and off the ship, at their dining table, shaking hands with the captain, birthday parties. The walls were festooned with ribbons of photographs, taken on every occasion. The photographers were an industrious team.

'Would you mind putting this into one of your nice envelopes, sealing it and stamping it with the date?' I asked one of the assistants behind the counter. She must have thought I was mad. It still wasn't foolproof but it was the best I could think of on the spur. They could still say I picked it up ages ago.

I sat down at a table that was hidden by a large fern, took out my notebook and began writing.

1. Joanna is not dead.
2. She did not fall overboard. Only her bathrobe fell overboard.
3. She has recovered from her shock trance.
4. She knew Berry had locked me in the stateroom.
5. She has an accomplice/friend on board called Ollie.
6. She is going to get herself a new identity. Why?
7. She wants to get things moving. What things moving?

I stared at my notes. As often happens, another thought strayed into my head. The invisible man, the one in the background of all the CCTV film. A mystery man that no one recognized. That was Ollie.

I strolled back to the photo salon and walked slowly past all the hundreds and hundreds of couple photographs, smiling, smiling, smiling, from the wall. Why do we all smile into a camera even if our heart is breaking? When I was almost cross-eyed with faces, I spotted a snap of him coming down the gangway, behind another smiling couple, wrapped up in scarves and caps at Tromso who had stopped to pose at the end of the gangway. He looked grim-faced, determined not to be photographed, already shaking his head.

I unpinned the photo and took it to the counter. I put on my fluttery, dizzy old lady expression. 'My dear, do you have any idea who this gentleman is? He's very much like someone I used to know. It would be lovely to say hello again.'

The photo was passed round the staff. 'Sorry,' said the girl. 'We don't know his name. We've never seen him or taken his photograph by request. One of those shrinking violets. Not everyone wants their photo taken. Perhaps he's a celebrity or on the run.'

'Thank you, dear. I'll put the photo back on display for you, shall I? You're so busy.'

'Thank you.'

As soon as she was occupied with a customer, I slid the photo into my bag. I'm such a liar.

Where was James? I needed to talk to him, tell him what I had found out, that I had seen Joanna Carter. Show him the photograph. Get his opinion. I had not seen him for hours. I'd seen everyone else, practically the entire passenger list.

We were still aground. No one seemed to be doing anything. The birds were the most active. Still agitated and distressed. Perhaps we ought to throw them a few bread rolls.

'We could rock the ship off, like they did in that Caribbean pirate film,' I suggested to a video man who hung over the rail taking shots of waves. 'You know, run from one side to the other, all of us. Rock it.'

'You into that kinda film, grandma?' came the laconic reply.

'I was in it,' I said, flipping one hundred per cent. He was so rude. 'Don't you recognize the mask? I came up from the depths of the wreck with a crab in my mouth.'

'I should take it out if I were you.'

James rescued me. 'Is my aunt troubling you?' he said, taking my arm a little too firmly. 'She gets overexcited about things and it's time for her medicine.'

He led me away, talking in a consoling manner. 'Come along, auntie. Time for your nice medicine. Then you can have a sweetie afterwards. You'd like that, wouldn't you?'

I could barely control my laughter. I turned it into a fit of asthmatic coughing. James was holding me up now. His eyes were brimming with mirth. At that moment, I had never loved him more. He was my star, my hero, my always everyman.

'A j–jelly baby?' I managed to choke out.

'You can have two. Promise.'

'Pink ones?'

'Any colour you like.'

He led me down some steep stairs to a lower deck and then towards the stern of the ship where it was more private. He pulled me into the shadowy space between two lifeboats and put his mouth against my ear. I could feel his breath fanning my skin. For one dizzy moment, I thought he was going to kiss me, but no. He didn't. He was speaking in a low voice.

'What's this all about? How has Berry found the bird has flown? What's this good news he has for you?'

'It's a trick,' I whispered back. 'He's trying to trick me into giving myself up. So I'm stuck as Miss Brown for ever and ever. I'm getting quite itchy in these stage clothes. Come closer. I've something to tell you.' I pulled him to me. I had never done this before. It was heady stuff. He smelled delicious, fresh not floral. 'Guess what? I've seen Joanna Carter.'

He pulled away. 'Are you all right?'

'Yes, in the flesh. Joanna Carter is alive and well. I didn't kill her. I'm totally innocent as I always was.'

'Tell me about it.'

So I told him about seeing her through a crack in the door hinge. I told him everything she said. He nodded a few times.

'This doesn't surprise me,' he said. 'I thought all along that it was some sort of con, a swindle, a scam. But I couldn't see what was happening and why they had set you up to take the blame. It's coming clear because I have found out the identity of the grey man. His name is Oliver Carter.'

'Joanna's husband,' I breathed.

'Yes, he's also a passenger on the ship. So he must be involved.'

'So is Berry and maybe even Dr Russell. Though he is rather nice when he's in a good mood.'

'And you've been around when he's been in a good mood?'

He was teasing me in the gentlest way. He knew that we were an item even if neither of us planned to do anything about it.

'Yes,' I said, nodding. 'He was in a good mood several times. It bolstered my morale immediately. And, I can tell you, sometimes it needs bolstering. Especially when I'm feeling abandoned.'

'This kind of bolstering?' he asked. He kissed me, softly and sweetly, folding his arms round me. Time stood still as it does when history is being made. He eased away slowly. 'I'll get a reputation if I'm seen kissing my maiden aunt.'

'Your maiden aunt could do with this kind of medicine three times a day.'

'And the jelly babies?'

'Lay in a stock.'

He pressed a key card into my hand. 'This is the spare

key to my cabin. It's twin-bedded, so no maidenly hysterics please. Use it as you wish. Sleep when you want to. Have a shower. Help yourself to tea, coffee, hot chocolate.'

The invitation saved me from curling up behind the curtains in the lounge. I tried not to think about the sharing aspect. Head firmly on shoulders, girl.

I took the photo out of my bag. 'Here's a photograph of Oliver Carter. If they are thinking of getting off at Bergen, we've got to move fast.'

'Impound her passport. Invalidate her swipe card – easy if she is supposed to be dead. She won't be able to get off unless she makes a run for it. I'll go and see the captain, though it might not be so easy. The ship is aground. He has other things on his mind.'

'Other things on my mind, too,' I said, wrapping my arms round him.

'Steady on, auntie. You haven't had your medicine.'

His inside twin-bedded cabin was perfect for two. None of the luxury of the two interconnecting staterooms on A Deck but all that anyone could need for comfortable sleeping, washing and relaxing.

His few possessions were in the wardrobe and one drawer. I had everywhere else for myself but nothing to put in it. But at least I could have a shower and use their shower gel.

As I stood in the shower, letting the warm water soothe my tense muscles, I thought of the problems in Latching that faced me. I had to find somewhere to live. Two weeks had nearly gone of the month's notice. My two bedsits were not overfurnished. Many items could be stored at FCI premises, till I found my dream home. The books were more of a headache. I had more books than were sensible for one pair of eyes.

I turned off the water, dried myself on a big towel and put on James's own navy blue towelling robe that hung behind the door. It was big on me but I wrapped the extra folds round and tied the belt. It didn't take long to make a cup of coffee from the hospitality tray. I stretched out on the second bed and let my tired bones relax. If I closed my eyes, I would be asleep in seconds.

At least I felt safe in James's cabin, the first time for days. Motivation, motivation, motivation. There must be a motive for Joanna wanting to lay the blame for her death on me.

I could write one of those outrageous confessional features for a woman's magazine with a screaming coverline: Wealthy Woman frames Best Friend for her own Murder. They pay very well, I understand. Joanna had plenty of glossy photographs I could use and there were those sketches. Portfolio for murder.

What usually happened when wealthy people died? Firstly, they leave their estate, i.e. money, to someone, usually family. But often they have huge life insurance which is paid out on death. Death has to be saintly or proved. And death has to be by accident or intent. And murder is certainly intent. An insurance policy would have an invalidity clause about suicide.

Supposing they were all in it? Geoff Berry, Max Russell, Joanna and Oliver Carter. Supposing they were going to split the spoils four ways in unequal amounts? Joanna and Oliver would go off into the sunset, hand in hand, with a tidy capital sum in their joint bank account and a villa in the Bahamas. Berry would buy himself a second pension. Max would buy . . . well, I had no idea.

But why me? Why not? They had to have some idiot to frame for the murder. Who better than a small town private eye with money problems and a reputation for getting her investigations in a twist. How could I have been so naive? But there had been nothing to make me suspicious. The threats on her life had seemed genuine. Yet Joanna could easily have slipped out while she was making that coffee, and hung the noose on the tree.

I heard the door opening. I turned over on to my side, a smile of welcome ready for James.

'I thought I'd find you here, Jordan. Especially when I discovered that DI James was once operational at Latching

CID. Your paths must have crossed during your various investigations. And crossed they obviously did. That looks a lot like a man's towelling robe. What else will DI James be lending you?'

Geoff Berry was standing in the doorway, looking so smug and triumphant. I thought of throwing the coffee in his face but what good would that have done? I could hardly run around the ship half naked.

'You're not going to escape this time. I'm going to make sure you don't get out again. I've put a guard on the door and I'm having the lock combination changed first thing. Not even your fancy man will be able to get you out.'

'I don't have a fancy man,' I said coldly.

'And I'll take all these clothes, if you can call them clothes.' He scooped up the pile of granny gear off the chair with distaste. 'Now give me your key.'

'I don't have one,' I said. 'DI James let me in.'

DI James's key was in the electricity socket by the door which activated the lights. It was there for all the world to see. But Geoff hadn't noticed.

'I'm getting the lock changed so DI James won't be able to get in and you won't be able to get out.'

Geoff Berry was too hyped up with this chain of success to check on my latest lie. His face was red with excitement. His next move would be handcuffs.

He slammed the door shut and I was alone again. It had all happened so quickly. I could barely believe it. There was no point in protesting that Joanna Carter was alive and no charge would stick on me. I'd have to prove it and if Berry was involved, he'd make sure that was impossible.

There was no way out. If I took the side off the bath, the space was about big enough for an outsize rabbit to hop along. And where would it lead to? If I took off the ventilation screen in the ceiling, it would be big enough for a couple of mosquitoes. There was no porthole, and they were firmly fixed to the ship, anyhow. How was I going to get out this time?

I sat on the edge of the bed, contemplating my fate. My hand was on the keys of the bedside telephone. I keyed in a familiar set of numbers.

'Hello,' I said, all sweetness and light. 'Room service, please?'

TWENTY-ONE

Still Aground

I walked smartly down the corridor, pushing the trolley of covered dishes. I looked clean and pristine in the steward's uniform, my hair pulled tightly back into a bun like a ballet dancer. Well, I had just had a shower.

The guard smiled at me and helped himself to a stick of celery from a serving dish. 'She all right in there?' he asked.

'Right as rain,' I said. 'Tucking into her meal.'

'Hope she saves some for me.'

'Ask her nicely in about an hour's time.'

I continued pushing the serving trolley down the corridor. A cabin door opened abruptly and a woman put her head round the door. Her hair was wound up in jumbo rollers, her face covered in a rapidly drying green mask which made it difficult for her to talk.

'Steward,' she said stiffly. 'Will you bring me a bottle of rosé?'

'Of course, madam. Australian, French or Portuguese?' My hand went into the jacket uniform pocket. The pad and pen were there. 'Your cabin number, please?'

'It's on the door,' she snapped. 'Portuguese rosé.'

There was the number on the door. This was a doddle. 'And your name, please?'

'Lesser. Mrs Lesser. And a pot of coffee and make sure it's hot,' she added.

'Yes, madam. I'll make sure it's hot. Caff or decaff?'

'I don't care. Just bring me some coffee.'

I was really quite good at this but I hoped that no more customers would come flocking to my little order pad. The serving trolley was cumbersome and I dumped it in the first stewards' kitchen that I came across.

Somehow I had to find DI James without attracting too much attention.

I picked up a small tray and sallied forth into the thirsty world. The lounge was my first port of call. A thick sea mist had rolled in and the lounge was packed with travellers who were not going anywhere. It was almost impossible to see out of the windows. The mist was white, licking the windows, like in a vampire film.

'Steward, over here, two coffees please.'

'Yes, sir. What kind of coffee?'

'Latte.' The passenger offered his cruise card and I wrote down his name and cabin number on the order pad. I had a feeling he was going to wait a long time for those two lattes. I hoped he wasn't too thirsty.

I took several more orders. I was so efficient, except that I dare not go to the bar with the orders because I would be instantly recognized or rather not recognized as a genuine member of the hotel staff. A drawback. There might be some sort of alert.

I went out on to the deck holding the tray and a bright smile and was immediately swallowed by the mist. It felt cold and clammy. My face was damp and tiny beads of moisture clung to my hair. It was like being submerged.

It was actually dangerous to be walking on deck and crewmen were closing the deck doors and putting no entry ropes across the handles. The *Orpheus* was still not moving and now that no one could see anything, there was a feeling of isolation and growing panic. Even the bird island was lost to view. All the novelty of the situation had worn off. Passengers wanted to be moving.

James might go back to his cabin and demand to be let in. He'd find the steward in his underpants, eating my order and watching a DVD. I said he could. He only had to stay there an hour or so. It was all part of a crazy job-swopping bet and I promised him twenty pounds if I won. He was already writing a letter home on the complimentary cabin stationery.

A man loomed out of the mist, order at the ready.

'One brandy, one American ginger ale, one cup of tea,

no sugar, portion of honey, two sandwiches, one ham and tomato, the other cream cheese and iceberg lettuce, two yogurts, one plain, one strawberry and a packet of crisps. Oh yes, and some walnuts. Have you got all that, steward?'

'Yes, sir. Any mayonnaise on the sandwiches? Where would you like it served?'

'Out here on deck. I don't like my conversations being overheard. And don't drop the tray coming back. It might roll overboard. We don't want to be charged for a lost tray.'

I couldn't see him properly but I knew the voice. He had found me as I knew he would. It was James. Pity about the order.

'How did you find me?'

'A woman in a cabin near mine said she'd ordered rosé wine and a pot of coffee about half an hour ago and it still hadn't come. She said the steward had red hair and was a complete idiot. So I knew it was you.'

He was not laughing at me though I could barely see his face. He drew me into the shelter of a pile of sun loungers. He took off his sweater and draped it over my shoulders.

'They just can't get the staff these days,' I said.

'You'd better put this on,' he said.

'Berry locked me in your cabin, took away my clothes and put a guard on the door.'

'He sure is a tough cookie.'

'I've nowhere to go any more.' I was near to tears or perhaps it was mist settling on my face. 'That man's out to get me. When he discovers I've disappeared again . . .'

'He won't. We've a lot to go on now. You say that Joanna is alive and planning to get off in Bergen. And we are going to solve this mystery. Forget the so called security officer. You are going to stay with me. I won't let you out of my sight for a single minute.'

And I believed him. Not out of his sight for a single minute.

'We need to draw Joanna Carter out of hiding somehow.

You think she's in Oliver Carter's cabin most of the time,' he went on. 'We have to get her out and her cover blown. Maybe an emergency, a fire drill, muster stations, something urgent. But that's rather dramatic and not fair on the other passengers. It's got to be something that relates only to Joanna.'

'Berry and the doctor are both involved, although I'm not sure how.'

'A message from the two of them, perhaps. Let's think along those lines. We need bait.'

'Don't look at me.'

He wasn't listening to me. 'You'd be the perfect bait. She'd come out if it was something to do with you. After all, you could ruin all her plans, whatever they are at this stage.'

'I won't do it.'

'Come on, Jordan. You know it makes sense.'

'It might make sense but it wouldn't work. She'd send along her henchmen, one with a truncheon and the other with a hypodermic needle. I'd be fish fodder in five minutes.'

'You do have a gruesome turn of phrase, Jordan. OK, we'll think of something else. But it had better be quick. As soon as we are off this unexpected underwater obstacle, we'll be heading for the port of Bergen.'

'And we could lose her forever once there. They could fly anywhere in the world. But I do have an idea.'

'I've been dreading those words. Your ideas are usually crack-brained and totally unworkable.' James tried to stifle a groan. The mist swirled round him like a wraith.

'Supposing we send her a note saying we've caught her new image on CCTV and we've had a copy of the film made and we want to meet her somewhere to discuss terms to our mutual benefit, i.e. it's blackmail. We'd blackmail her.'

'She'd probably guess it was us. She's pretty devious.'

I heard the slightest rustle of clothes nearby. A sniff and a cough. Someone cleared their throat.

'But she wouldn't guess if the message came from me,'

said a voice I recognized, a contralto voice bubbling with excitement. 'Now I've been listening to every word so I've an idea who you're talking about. Mrs Joanna Carter, the poor woman tied on to the keelhauling ladder. Of course, I would like to be filled in on the greyer areas.'

She loomed out of the mist like a polar bear treading an ice flow. It was Natasha in her trademark fur coat, swathed in scarves and dangling earrings. Her eyes were bright with enthusiasm.

'Do let me help. I'm so bored. There's not a decent man under fifty on this ship and I've read all the books in the library, seen all the films. The bridge club have had me banned for talking and there's absolutely nothing to do. Except eat and I don't want to do any more of that.'

'Natasha, how lovely to see you,' and I really meant it. She was a friendly face from last week. 'So much has happened. James, this is Natasha. We were on the same table in the dining room, many years ago, it seems.'

'James,' said Natasha, looking at him with open admiration. He didn't move or seem to notice. His face was dark and still. 'James is such a nice name. The only decent man aboard and I can see that he's already taken. Pity. Never mind, perhaps Jordan will let me share. Occasionally.'

'It's not like that, Natasha,' I said quickly, disturbed by her eye-swivelling towards James. He gave no sign of being worried by her attention. 'But your help might go a long way to solving this terrible situation. Perhaps we ought to talk about it a bit more.'

'I want to know everything. Please tell me. You can trust me.'

'Jordan has been framed.' said James. 'It's as simple as that. We want to get Joanna out of hiding. To prove that she's alive.'

'That's exactly what we'll do. It'll be my pleasure to get you out of this mess, Jordan. Just tell me what I have to do and I'll do it. That po-faced security officer is a pompous ass and needs to be taught a lesson. As for that dishy doctor, I don't know what's gotten into him lately. It's like he's been infected with one of his own diseases.'

'It's very strange,' I agreed. 'He's completely changed. He used to be so nice.'

A low booming sound came out of the mist. We stopped talking and listened intently. It was ghostly. Natasha went pale beneath her make-up. The sound came again and she clutched at my arm. She had lost her nerve.

'Jordan, what is it? What's that awful noise? Is the ship sinking?'

'I think that's a pair of tugs coming to pull us off the sea bed. Nothing to worry about, Miss Natasha,' said James. 'This might be a good moment to take cover before everyone comes out to watch the event. We can't go to my cabin. Berry has put a guard on the door.'

'Welcome to my cabin, one deck down,' said Natasha, recovering. 'And we'll find you something a little more attractive to wear, Jordan. That steward's uniform is not exactly flattering. It's meant to fit a lanky young man. And I've a bottle of gin that needs opening in good company. Drinking alone is the first step to becoming an alcoholic.'

Passengers were flocking back to the decks to watch the arrival of the tugs. We followed Natasha to her cabin. She had a double bed cabin for single occupancy. I suppose she needed the extra room for her vast wardrobe.

She shut the door firmly and went straight to the refrigerator. 'My steward has remembered to bring fresh ice, thank goodness. Just what we need to sharpen the brain. A double G & T.' She poured out large drinks, no pub measures here. She seemed to have plenty of glasses, no doubt ferried back to her cabin on different evenings.

'Cheers,' she said.

'Cheers,' I said, wondering what on earth was going to happen now. One minute I was being charged with murder, the next drinking a large double gin and tonic in a passenger's cabin. I wondered what she was going to find me to wear. She was twice my size.

'Your hospitality is very generous,' said James, helping

himself to a beer and prising off the cap. He took a deep drink. 'But first things first. This is what we are going to do.'

'I'm going to like this,' said Natasha, looking at James.

TWENTY-TWO

At Sea

Sometime before midnight, another tug arrived and the two powerful engines carefully eased the *Orpheus Odyssey* off the ground bank with ropes attached to her stern. It was a delicate manoeuvre. I watched from the promenade deck in borrowed crew fatigues. It was baggy round the waist but then James would have little knowledge of my vital statistics.

'Keep a low profile,' he said.

'OK,' I said. 'I won't join the sail away party on deck.'

'If you are nice to me, I might bring you a glass of bubbly.'

'How nice?'

'Well, quite nice. No playground tears, please.'

That was the limit of our flirtation but it was a good start. I flashed him a saucy smile but he had already gone. It was always the way. James would rescue me from some situation and then go.

Natasha had also vanished somewhere. She had been quickly primed as to how she should approach Joanna Carter. It was all such flimsy evidence. I wondered how she was going to manage.

'Phone Oliver Carter's cabin and make an arrangement to meet Joanna at some discreet spot but somewhere clearly in public view,' said James. 'The shop might be a good place. You could make your financial proposition to her while examining a rail of sparkling party clothes.'

'My favourite place. They have plenty of things in my size,' Natasha laughed.

'But don't go anywhere with her,' I said. 'You can't trust her.'

'I'll be careful. Don't you worry. I can handle Mrs Carter.'

How could anyone handle Mrs Carter? She was devious in every possible way. She would trick her own grand-mother.

Could we rely on this effervescent woman to carry out our hoax, without giving us away? It was the way she said, so confidentially, 'I can handle Mrs Carter,' that worried me. Then it struck like a blow to the solar plexus. She could be part of a double double-cross and was another of Joanna's planted accomplices. Maybe they would all walk away with a share of the pay-out. She could buy another fur coat.

But it was too late for a change of plan.

'I'll be nearby,' James went on. 'At some point, I'll make myself known and escort her to the captain on the bridge. He's the only one on board who can actually arrest her and put her in custody. Apparently there is a cadet's cabin which can be made totally secure.'

'How did you find that out?' I asked.

'I'm a detective, remember?'

I wanted to go home. Another wave of homesickness threatened my stability. I longed for the pier at Latching on its wobbly legs, the seagulls, Maeve's Café, my friends, the beach. Especially the beach and the churning waves. I felt no connection now to this different sea, this ship and this deck above the sea.

It was a relief to feel the ship moving again. The captain had a lot of time to make up and nautical miles to cover before we docked in Bergen. Every mile covered now was a mile nearer Latching. We were returning, on our way home.

We were going home.

James had left me with nothing to do. I could hardly hang about in crew gear, admiring the view. Some diligent sideways searching produced a J-cloth, lifted from a steward's service trolley while he was in a cabin delivering clean towels. I decided to clean everywhere.

I took the J-cloth and diligently began polishing every brass rail or knob or handle in sight. There were plenty of them. I kept my head down and moved around the ship like a busy beaver. I'd be getting a service award at this rate.

An officer stopped me. 'Hey, lad. What are you doing?' he asked.

I pointed to my ear and shook my head, feigning total deafness. I also managed a pathetic smile. He looked puzzled, obviously trying to place the deaf crew youngster whose name he could not recall.

'OK, boy. Carry on.'

'Yes, sir.'

Promenade deck soon shone like a lighthouse. It was time for me to move on downwards towards the Scheherazade shop of delights. Natasha would have contacted Joanna by now. She might even be negotiating how much money was going to change hands.

I saw Francis Guilbert coming towards the stairs. He must be wondering what had happened to me as I hadn't spoken to him for some time. Then he stopped and turned towards the photo shop, obviously going to hand in a film for them to process. It was a poignant moment. I would have to make it up to him, too, sometime. It seemed I owed a lot of people.

There was a moment of hesitation. I could explain to Francis now and make things clear. But someone pushed in front of me and the opportunity was lost.

I nipped into the Clarus cinema in polish mode but found little made of brass inside. Also I could barely see in the dark. My eyes were curtained until they adjusted. I stopped for a second, always happy to watch Hugh Grant doing a Prime Ministerial boogie along the corridors of No. 10. They were showing *Love Actually* again for passengers who were tired of watching mist.

They were not in the shop. It was busy with browsing passengers but there was no sign of Natasha or Joanna Carter conversing over some clothes rail. Not even the bargain sale rail. I began to feel a rise of panic. I couldn't stay. Crew were not allowed in the shop unless it was to repair something.

The stairs were empty. First sitting had started and a surge of passengers were filling the Delphi dining room, using the antiseptic squirt at the entrance. I had forgotten the time of day or what it was like to eat normally.

Natasha was nowhere. Joanna Carter was probably ordering à la carte room service with wine. I felt an anger, flat and sharp, that wiped out previous concern about Natasha or Joanna. What were they doing? Where was Natasha? I phoned her cabin, using the service phone but there was no answer.

I began a systematic search of the ship, keeping a low profile, polishing anything in sight, including wooden fixtures and fire extinguishers.

James was also nowhere to be seen. But it was so easy to miss anyone on board, all those decks, all those different routes via stairs and lifts. It was a wonder that passengers ever met the person they were sharing a cabin with. Hey, have we met? Are we sharing? That's my bed.

The women had disappeared completely. It was normally easy to spot Natasha, huge and flamboyant and flowing, glowing like a beacon. But the light had gone out.

Where was the last place anyone would look for Natasha? The thought hovered in my mind, then I knew. She did not exercise.

The gym.

She would never be seen among all that monster wall machinery and two mirrored walls that reflected back any personal grossness with total honesty. It was the last place on earth or sea that she would go to. I pressed the button in the lift down into the depths of the ship, the place where people came to work off their last meal.

The corridors were less plush. This was where people worked out or took their smalls to the laundry. A smell of sweat lingered in the air. The machines were motionless. It was empty. The pool water swished from side to side accommodating the swell. Should I stay or should I leave? It was like that crucial moment in the film *Sliding Doors*.

I turned to leave but heard a sudden whirring noise behind me.

The watertight doors were closing.

They were heavy white steel walls that could close in seconds in an emergency. I ran towards them but hesitated, remembering being told about an awful incident when a crew member did exactly the same and had an arm severed. I needed both arms.

That moment of hesitation was my downfall. It was a failure of monumental proportion, the beginning of a nightmare. I had forgotten where I was. Was anything going to kick in?

The doors clanged shut. Watertight doors? Was this an emergency? What emergency? Had we hit another bit of shallow ground? Had the hull been holed? Was I trapped in a watertight compartment?

I stood watching the waves slapping the sides of the pool. We were still moving. My heart took on a wilder beat, praying that it was a drill of some sort, testing all the doors, and that this one would open soon.

But nothing happened. There was no one else around. No evidence of staff. I went to the desk to use the phone but the connection had been severed. Then I switched on the computer but it was dead. The screen was blank. I couldn't even check my emails.

I was trapped. It was not a happy moment.

TWENTY-THREE

Still at Sea

The pockets of the crew fatigues yielded nothing. No handy gadget for opening watertight steel doors. No packet of chocolate biscuits. No chewing gum. Me and my J-cloth were totally isolated.

I wandered round the equipment in the gymnasium, wondering if the weights could be used, but I could hardly lift anything heavier than the one kilo pair. Two weeks of cruising and my muscles had gone to flab. There was another computer on the manicurist's treatment table but that was also dead. Whoever had turned this into a living grave had made a thorough job of it.

Time to phone a friend. I dialled Hamish's mobile number but there was no answer. Either it was switched off or needed recharging. Perhaps he had to switch it off when he was on the bridge because of the delicate navigational instruments.

The forward end of the ship and this far down in the depths was completely sealed in. I could practically feel the point. No daylight of any kind, no corridors leading to somewhere else. It was like the last drawer in a refrigerator where things get forgotten.

'Of course, it's the swell,' I said aloud to myself. 'They have closed the doors because of the swell, being careful.' There was stillness and emptiness, only the slapping of the pool water. 'Or perhaps it's shallow water again.'

I stopped. There was the faintest scratching sound, like a mouse running along a skirting board. Rats. Supposing there were rats this far down? But surely not on such a beautiful, well-kept, pin-clean floating palace? No discounts for rats.

It came again. The faintest scratching. I began to listen

carefully, to trace the noise to its source. It seemed to come from the changing rooms, tucked away to the side. The doors were closed but opened to my touch.

There were lockers for clothes and a shower and toilet. Further on was another door marked SAUNA.

The sound was coming from the sauna. I looked around for a weapon. A bowl of fresh fruit was hardly a weapon. I shook out a big towel and advanced into the sauna, holding it up against my face, ready to swamp anything that attacked me, like a survivor from Davy Jones's locker.

A blast of heat hit me. The sauna was going at full steam ahead. I could barely see for the mist rising from the artificial hot coals. The temperature was unbearable. A tropical jungle.

A mountain of flesh was sprawled on the lower bench, naked, strapped to the wood with wide brown parcel tape. The same tape was stretched across her mouth and her eyes. Her nails were making this faint noise of movement on the wood. Sweat was running off her body in rivulets. She was melting in the heat.

It was Natasha. I didn't wait for modesty but pulled the tape off her mouth first, then threw the towel over her body. Then I eased the tape off her eyes. She lost a lot of eyelashes. Fortunately, most of them were false.

Her eyes were petrified with fear, staring. Then she saw it was me and a flash of relief filled them. She began to struggle, dripping with sweat.

'Keep still, Natasha,' I said. 'You're safe now but you need water first.'

A row of water bottles were conveniently displayed in the gym and I grabbed a couple off a shelf, unscrewing the lids. Back in the sauna, I poured some into Natasha's mouth and she swallowed greedily, drinking, drinking. The manicurist's workplace revealed a pair of scissors and I raced back with them, freeing her wrists, her arms and legs and ankles, cutting off the tape. She sat up gratefully, still drinking, clutching the towel to her heaving bosom.

'Jordan,' she gasped. 'They did it. They did it . . . I thought I was going to die. They were leaving me here to die.'

'I'm so sorry,' I said, helping her out of the sauna and on to one of the loungers round the pool. She fell on to it, all huddled up, still catching her breath. 'We wouldn't have asked you to help if we thought there was any danger. Who did it? Tell me slowly.'

She began to cry. Every bit of her body wobbling. It was a sad sight. I found another big towel and gave it to her. She mopped up tears and sweat, drinking and spilling water and crying. It was a very wet scene.

'Joanna agreed to pay me for the photos and said we would go back to her cabin and she would get the money,' Natasha went on, still weeping. 'But she didn't. And there was this other man, in a uniform.'

'A khaki uniform?'

'I think so. I'm not sure. Not a regular crew uniform. It was that security officer. I only saw him for a second before they flung something over my head and bundled me down here.'

'It wasn't the doctor, Dr Russell?'

'Oh no, it wasn't the doctor.' She picked up a peach from the bowl and sank her teeth into the sweetness. She was obviously feeling better. 'I would know the doctor anywhere. I've spoken to him several times.'

'Tell me exactly what happened from the beginning.'

'I phoned the cabin and spoke to Joanna Carter. I told her I had photographs of her in a bar, talking to the doctor, when she was supposed to be overboard and declared missing and dead. I said I was prepared to give her the photographs and negatives for a very healthy sum of money.'

'How much did you ask for?'

'A hundred thousand pounds.'

'How much? A hundred thousand.' I nearly fell off the lounger. I was tucking into an apple now. Call it second sitting.

'Not a lot when you know that her life was insured for half a million and her husband would get the entire amount on her death. Quite a hefty windfall. They could live in style when it all quietened down, Bermuda, the Bahamas, Barbados.'

I choked on a bit of apple. My fifty thousand pounds was beginning to look like small change. I'd been set up to look as if I had murdered Joanna, so that they could claim the insurance. Somehow they made it appear that Joanna had been pushed overboard, when in fact only her white towelling robe had actually hit the sea. No one saw her body swallowed by the waves. She only had to lay low.

'What happened then?'

'They must have knocked me out with something, then bundled me into a lift and then I came to and found myself in this sauna, strapped to the bench without any clothes.' She began to cry again and I patted her arm. Her clothes must be somewhere. There were bins around for used towels. I found her clothes stuffed into the bottom of a bin.

She clutched the colourful bundle to her bosom gratefully. 'Thank you, thank you, Jordan.'

'I can't tell you how sorry I am that you got involved. It was unforgivable of us. There was too much danger, too much risk. But please tell me how you know that they took out insurance for half a million on Joanna's life? It's not something they were likely to tell you.'

'I have a confession to make,' said Natasha, searching in the fruit bowl for another peach. 'I'm not who you think I am. Yes, my name is Natasha, but I am actually a claims investigator for the insurance company involved. It is a very large sum for a couple to take out and there was no reciprocal policy on the husband's life. That always makes us suspicious. I needed a holiday anyway.'

'So you have been watching Joanna all the time, and me as well, I suppose?'

'Yes, dearie, at first I thought you were involved, but then I realized you had nothing to do with it. The whole scheme was far more complicated and you were being set up.'

'What made you think that?'

'It was the incident of the diamond necklace at the captain's cocktail party. You see, I saw Joanna take off the necklace and slip it to a man. I followed the man and saw him put it in the used towel bin.'

'Her husband? Oliver Carter, the grey man.'

'Yes, I'm sure it was, now. But if you had been in on the scheme, then she would have slipped it to you, far easier, and you would have put it in the towel bin. So I knew from the start that you were a complete innocent.'

'What about the keelhauling, Joanna being strapped to the ladder? That really happened, didn't it?'

'I don't think it did. Everything below is kept locked at all times. There is no way that anyone could be strapped to the ladder. But there is a way of getting Joanna on to one of the maintenance platforms, securely bound in luggage straps and pretending that she had been rescued from the ladder. I think Geoff Berry had a lot to do with stage managing that event.'

'Then Berry is involved?'

'Up to his neck. Beware of the man. A nasty individual.'

'I know. He was the reason I was sacked from the police.'

Natasha sent me a look of sympathy. She was obviously worn out and looked years older without make-up. Her time in the sauna had exhausted her. She only wanted to rest and sleep.

'I think I'll go back to my cabin now and have a nice shower and a generous gin and tonic. I could sleep,' Natasha said, gathering all her things together.

Now for the bad news. 'Unfortunately we can't get out, Natasha. Someone has closed the watertight doors. No prizes for guessing who. And no one knows we are down here.'

'Phone someone for help.'

'The phones are dead. And the computers. We can't even send an email.'

She collapsed like an expired balloon. There was nothing I could say or do to cheer her up. I needed cheering up too.

'At least we have the bowl of fruit, plenty of water, the loungers and a cupboard full of clean towels. We'll make ourselves comfortable and wait it out.'

'I'm supposed to be going to drinks this evening,' said Natasha.

'Perhaps they'll miss you and send out a search party.'

'Your dishy DI should be sending out a search party.'

'He probably is,' I said with more confidence that I really felt. DI James had rescued me from many disasters but this felt different. He was not on his home ground. 'I've checked all the phones and all the computers. They have been severed or disconnected. We have no contact with the outside world.'

'How are we going to let them know that we are stuck down here?'

'I don't know,' I said glumly.

'If I can't have a shower, then I'm going to have a swim,' said Natasha. She threw off the towels and plunged into the pool like a white whale. It was an awesome sight. But I had to admire her. She was grossly overweight but her body told her she needed cooling down, to swim in water, and that was what she was going to do.

I struggled out of the crew fatigues. At least I was wearing bra and pants, two items more than Natasha. I dived into the water and it was cool and refreshing and for one blissful moment I could forget that someone was trying to kill me.

I came up for air. Natasha was paddling about, water streaming off her hair. She did not look as if she was about to duck my head under water. I was still not a hundred and one per cent sure of her. I took a deep breath and dived down again.

For some reason I thought the pool might have a plug. If I pulled the plug out and the pool emptied, surely this would register on some computer somewhere? Pools don't empty themselves. They'd send someone down to find out why.

There was no plug. Of course it wouldn't have a plug. It was not a bath.

I came up, gasping. Somewhere there must be a valve. I tried to remember something, anything about swimming pools. How to fill them. How to empty them. That area of my education had been neglected. Usually it was done by bronzed young pool men, flexing their muscles. It was probably on line, by computer these days.

I began hunting around for anything that looked like a valve.

The swell was making the water slosh about, drenching the walls. Natasha was clinging to the ladder that led out of the pool, trying to stop herself from falling off.

'I think I'm coming out,' she said. 'It's getting a bit rough for me.'

'Any idea of how to empty this pool?'

'Drink it?'

Her humour had returned.

'Would it be a valve or a pump?'

'I'd go for a pump.'

'Have you seen anything that looks like a pump?'

She was climbing out, shaking her head. She'd got water in her ears. I handed her some towels. We were going through their stock of towels at a rate of knots. I looked at the pile of wet towels for inspiration. They needed washing. Was there a laundry chute?

I started a systematic search of the entire area, gym, sauna, changing rooms and pool. Nothing. They obviously collected used towels in bags to deliver to the laundry. I began my search again, this time tapping on every surface. There must be something I had missed.

The changing rooms each had a wall of lockers, a row of hooks on another wall, a shower and a lavatory. The last wall had a wooden bench. On the bench in the men's changing room was a navy Hessian bag, with drawstring neck. It was stuffed full of used towels. The men obviously used more towels than the women passengers.

I tapped on the wall above the bench. It had a different sound to the other walls. Had I found something? Was it going to be something useful, or merely a cupboard with shelves stacked with clean rolled-up towels? Under the end of the bench was the smallest lever. I pushed it towards the wall. A panel opened.

It was a lift, about the size of service lifts used in restaurants decades ago. It was for bags of laundry, that was obvious, and one bag was here, waiting to be delivered. But the bag could wait. The lift was going to deliver me.

There was no start button anywhere. It was my guess that it worked on weight.

I rushed back to Natasha. She was half asleep, wrapped up in towels.

'Stay here. I've found a way out but only one of us can go. I'll be back soon. Don't worry. Have a banana.'

TWENTY-FOUR

The Seven Mountains of Bergen

I t worked on weight. My weight. No sooner had I closed the door, than it began to descend. I was doubled over in the small space. It was pitch dark, like inside a mine. I was beginning to wish I'd found a pump.

I didn't know how many decks we went down. It felt like dozens. The laundry must be in the bowels of the ship, industrial sized machines churning out thousands of clean sheets, table napkins, tablecloths, towels, face flannels, pillowcases, non-stop, day in and night out.

Panic gripped me. Supposing the lift delivered the towels straight into a machine? But common sense told me that the bag would have to be emptied. The lift stopped, the door flap opened and, clever stuff, the floor of the inside tilted and tipped me into a large skip full of laundry bags. I floundered about, trying to stand, falling over, striving to regain some balance. The noise of the machines was thunderous. I needed earplugs.

I clung on to the edge, then realized I was wearing only a wet M & S bra and pants. Not suitable for this totally male regime. The laundry boys would be more panic-stricken than me. One of the drawstring necks was not firmly tied and I pulled out a crumpled pillowcase. I pulled it over my head and, with my teeth, tore at the other end, making a hole for my head. They could charge me.

Shopping list: buy replacement pillowcase. White.

I managed to climb out of the skip and half fell on to the floor. The area was a hive of industry. Not only huge washing machines, but huge tumble-dryers and vast ironing machines, clamping linen into pristine smoothness, thundered the air. They even had folding machines. And dozens of laundry crew in white gear hurried around, handling the

technical side of the laundry, and piling clean linen on to
trolleys. It was so well organized. I felt rather sorry to be
a cog in the wheels.

A dark-skinned boy caught sight of me and his eyes
widened. He stood shocked still.

'I wonder if I could use your phone?' I said.

'Where are you?' said James.

'I'm in the laundry.'

'I've been worried stiff.'

'And I've been worried stiff, and nearly starched stiff
down here. Trapped in the swimming pool, journey into
hell in the laundry lift, and now I'm in the laundry, about
to be folded and delivered to the dining room. And Natasha
is still trapped behind watertight doors at the pool, eating
her way through a bowl of fruit.'

'I don't understand a word of what you're saying. Start
again.'

'I'm not going to start again. You come down here and get
me. I'm not going anywhere without a police escort. Joanna
and her husband are trying to kill me, get rid of Natasha, and
skip the ship in Bergen. So we've got to move fast.'

'Don't move.'

'I'm hardly likely to in this outfit.'

I thanked the laundry manager for the use of his phone,
and waited for James to arrive. I was an object of much
curiosity and sly male grinning. They didn't get many female
visitors. A few tablecloths got folded into diagonal.

It felt like ages before James arrived. It was very hot in
the laundry and I was perspiring, my hair like string, all
decorum out the porthole, only there were no portholes that
far down, only ventilation shafts.

I saw him before he saw me. James was being escorted
through the maze of machines to where I was waiting, wall-
flower drooping by now, by the telephone. I had not moved
an inch. One of the boys had brought me a stool to sit on.

'So?' said James, not touching me. His eyes were their
usual glinting ocean depths. He did not look pleased to see
me. 'How am I going to explain this to the captain?'

'How are you going to explain the watertight doors to the captain?' I snapped back.

'No explanation yet but Natasha is safe and has been taken to the medical centre for a check-up. She's dehydrated. I had a few words with your dishy doctor friend and he seems much chastened. A woman called Flo Birley is keeping Natasha company.'

'That's good. Mrs Birley was on our table,' I said. 'I don't trust the doctor.'

'He says he's got something to tell you and to apologize.'

'Fat chance,' I said.

'Your debonair detective friend, Bill Quentin, has slapped Geoff Berry into a secure cabin, and is at present typing out a full report on Berry's computer.'

'Well done for Bill. One of the old sort. Totally trustworthy.'

'Francis Guilbert has asked me to give you a message that the champagne is on ice and Staff Captain Hamish Duncan is inviting you to dinner, when you've got cleaned up.'

James rocked back on his heels, still keeping his distance. 'There seems to be no end to your admirers.'

I felt a surge of satisfaction. 'Well, there you go,' I said. 'That's how to make friends and influence people on a cruise. It's not just a pretty face and a wardrobe full of posh clothes.'

He eyed the torn pillowcase with the first glimmer of relaxation on his face. Maybe he had been worried stiff in case I had gone to join the whales and been stung to death by a poisonous jelly fish.

'And what would you call that creation?' he asked.

'It's the Norwegian national costume,' I said. 'Only needs a few yards of braid.'

'Next time, perhaps you should make holes for your arms.'

I didn't know if it was day or night. I was quite surprised to go on deck and find it was a beautiful sunny morning and we were sailing parallel to the coast of Norway. The port of Bergen was ahead between ranges of mountains known as 'de syv fjell' or the Seven Mountains. Somewhere soon was the Stonj Bridge.

James draped his fleece over my shoulders. The temperature was not exactly warm, but I was so pleased to see the sun and sky, and all the colourful houses dotted along the coastline, that I didn't care if my toes were turning to ice.

He took a call on his mobile. 'Thank you,' he said. 'She'll be pleased to know that.' He turned to me. 'Your stateroom has been searched and cleared. It's safe for you to go back there, have a hot shower, get into your own clothes, order room service.'

'I can't go back,' I said. 'I'm too scared.'

'There's nothing for you to be scared of,' said James. 'Captain Armitage has arranged some excellent company for you. His wife joined the ship in Tromso. She says she'd be very happy to stay with you.'

'But what about Joanna Carter trying to do a runner in Bergen?'

'No way. Every single gangway, passenger and stores exit, will be guarded. The quay will be ringed with police cars. Unless they jump off the bridge with parachutes, they don't stand a chance of getting away. Don't worry, Jordan, we are going to find them before we reach Southampton. You enjoy the last few days of the cruise. You've earned some time off.'

I knew what I would wear that evening. It was my prime charity shop purchase, a tubular silk-crêpe pale pink dress with pearl beading. It was from the Thirties and had slipped past the scrutineers for vintage stock and on to the rails. It was beautiful and it fitted. I adored it. My fourth dress. In order, I now had a borrowed blue chiffon dress, a nearly new black shop dress, charity shop black chiffon evening dress and this silk-crêpe. My cup runneth over.

Max Russell came calling. He stood in the doorway, hesitating. 'May I come in, Jordan?' He was carrying a bunch of white roses. 'The nearest I could get to an olive branch.'

'Sorry, I'm a bit busy. Recovering from various traumas.'

'You should at least hear what he has to say,' said

Mrs Armitage. She was a pleasant woman, poised and authoritative, a veteran of cruises and cruising. 'I'll be on the balcony if you want me.'

Max came in and put the roses on the table. A white petal drifted to the floor.

'Like me,' he said. 'Coming apart.'

I said nothing to help. He did not look well. His good looks were also coming apart, cleft lines from nose to mouth, shadowed eyes. It had been a busy time in the medical centre. He needed some sleep.

I'd had a shower, was back in my blue track suit, hair drying loose.

'I have to apologize to you, Jordan, for being such a damned fool. I should have explained. I should have told you what was happening but it escalated so fast, I was caught up in it before I could get out of it.'

I relaxed fractionally. He sounded one hundred per cent confused. I still refused to say a word.

'Joanna's trance. It was all a fake, consummate acting. A charade, to get what she wanted, and eventually to fake her own murder. She blackmailed me into going along with it. I wish I'd said no. But I was panicked into agreeing. I didn't want to lose my job and –' he hesitated – 'my marriage.'

I allowed myself a long 'Aaahh.'

'I had become rather friendly with an unattached young woman on board, a senior officer. Nothing more than that, I assure you. Nothing happened really. But somehow Joanna found out and threatened to tell my wife and the captain. It seemed harmless at first, to pretend she was in a trance when she wasn't in a trance. I didn't know what she was planning to do to you.'

'What about Suna, the Thai stewardess?'

'Fixed, too. Sorry. Not genuine. She was provided by Geoff Berry. I don't know who she is or why. And the medication. It was planted by me. Sorry.'

'Despicable.'

'I know. I'm sorry the way I treated you. I could barely look at you afterwards, knowing how it was all a deceit. And when the feeding tube came out . . . well, it was always out when you weren't there. Joanna couldn't stand it. And, yes, she was eating grapes. I wish none of it had happened. I may have to resign.'

'So do you know where Joanna is hiding now?' I asked coldly.

'No, I've no idea and that's the truth.'

'And Natasha. Is she recovering from her ordeal?'

'She's doing fine. Sugar and water, milk and soup. She can return to the world of cruising sometime today. Natasha has nothing but praise for you. She thinks you are wonderful. The tops. Deserve a medal.'

It was soft soap. But I forgave him. Doctors worked hard, all hours, wherever they are and luxury cruise ships are no different.

'Don't resign,' I said suddenly. 'I shan't complain about your behaviour. Good doctors are hard to get.'

I got up and put the white roses into water. It was my gesture of forgiveness.

Bill Quentin was my next visitor. He also brought flowers. The bottled kind.

'We done good, girl,' he said. 'Pinned that bastard, Berry. He was in it up to his neck, sent you that nasty email. Do anything for money. I'll be sending a report in to West Sussex, get the record put straight. They might send you an apology.'

'I don't want to go back into the police.'

'You stay where you are. FCI sounds good. Give me a ring if you ever need a hand. This number will reach me anywhere in the world. I'd fancy some sea air.'

'Come any time you like,' I said. 'I'm looking for a new place. It might have a spare room. So what did you manage to get out of Berry?'

'It was a bit garbled since Berry wouldn't know how to put two words together. It seems that Joanna's life is insured for a cool half million. But there was a suicide clause, so it had to be murder. Natural causes being out of the question. She hired you to protect her but all the time setting you up as her murderer. Once you were arrested for her murder, devoted husband could put in the insurance claim and the pair of them would disappear into the far blue yonder.'

'So where is she now?'

Bill shook his head. 'Sorry. No idea.' Same phrase, different person.

Francis Guilbert came on the phone. 'I'm so relieved you are all right, Jordan. Will you have supper with me tonight in the dining room? You need a decent meal after all you've gone through, with excellent wine.'

'And good company,' I said.

'Will you come?

'Yes, of course. I'd love to. And I have the perfect pink dress, vintage. You'll love it.'

'That goes without saying.'

James was my last visitor. Mrs Armitage was getting bored with sitting on the balcony and went back to her husband's quarters on the bridge. But I thanked her warmly. She had been reassuringly normal.

James sat down and took in the roses and the bottle of malt whiskey. 'The admirers have been calling, I see,' he said.

'So kind, so generous,' I said, rubbing in that he had brought me nothing.

'I don't have any social graces,' he said. 'We have berthed alongside in Bergen. All is secure and the gangways are down. Health and safety checks completed. Do you want to go ashore? You need to stretch your legs especially after your journey in the laundry lift.'

'Thank you for reminding me, but no, I don't want to. I want to make sure that Joanna and her husband don't manage to get ashore, and make their escape to the airport.'

'The airport has been alerted.'

'So where are they? How are they going to get ashore?'

He stood up and held out his hands towards me. 'Suppose we go on deck, take in the air, and keep our eyes open?'

He clasped his hands over mine and pulled me up. His hands were firm and warm. We went on deck. I was walking on air. My blue track suit was warm enough for Bergen's icy air. It was such a pretty port, all the colourful seafront shops and cafés. The Seven Mountains in the distance. James kept hold of my hand in case I fell overboard.

We had mugs of hot chocolate on the lido deck, purely for the vitamin intake, keeping an eye on the passengers descending the gangway to the tour coaches or to walk independently round the town.

The sun was brilliant but the air was cold. A contradiction of terms. I could see the vernicular railway that took visitors up into the mountains. The views of the fjords would be marvellous but I was past views.

'There's Natasha,' I said. 'Look, there she is going down the gangway.'

It was easy to spot Natasha. She was wearing her huge fur coat, fur hat over eyes and flying scarves. A Goliath of a woman, slowly descending the gangway, testing each step.

'Max said she was recovering in the medical centre, so surely it's too soon for her to go sightseeing?'

James was up and away in seconds, flying to the side of the ship.

'Stop that woman,' he shouted into his mobile.

It was Joanna Carter, using Natasha's swipe card and wearing her clothes. She had helped herself to both while Natasha was in the sauna. But this time it was the Bergen police that took her away on the grounds of trying to illegally enter Norway. Not a monstrous crime but enough to keep her in custody till the fraud squad detectives flew over from the UK.

Oliver Carter was stopped later, leaving the ship on his own swipe card, but James was at the quayside, explaining why it was necessary that he should accompany his wife for questioning over a suspicious death.

'No argument, sir,' said James. 'We have sufficient evidence to charge you and your wife.'

'It was all her idea,' said Oliver Carter, white-faced.

'You'll have a chance to explain.'

'I had nothing to do with it. Joanna planned it all.'

'You are allowed one phone call.'

*   *   *

James came back on board ship a lot later. I didn't want to go ashore, even though Bergen's quayside warehouses looked so colourful and interesting. The Seven Mountains were snow-tipped, the snow glistening in the sunshine. I could hear music playing in the market place and the spirit of Grieg lived on, creating his wonderful piano concertos.

'You have all these invites and dinner dates from various admirers,' said James. 'So where have you decided you are spending the evening?'

I was wearing the pink silk-crêpe evening dress with the pearl beading. It was exquisite, perfect with my tawny hair. Same hair, washed and brushed out, fell down my back. I felt a different woman. I was wearing lashings of black mascara and some of Joanna's Dior perfume. Although her belongings had been confiscated, they had overlooked the perfume. No one was interested in the lipstick I'd labelled.

'There is only one person I want to be with,' I said. There, it was said. I waited for normal masculine put-down.

'Jordan,' James said, looking at me with renewed intent. 'I thought you would never ask.'

TWENTY-FIVE

Southampton

Captain Armitage was holding his early evening farewell cocktail party as we sailed the homeward straight through the North Sea. We'd passed many offshore oil platforms, some as far as thirty miles away, that could be seen because of their height above sea level.

It was quite windy with occasional rain showers but I didn't care if it rained. I only wanted to get home to Latching.

Except that would mean saying goodbye to James. He had to return to Yorkshire. I tried not to think about it, kept a smile fixed to my face. He was circulating with all the ease of a professional police officer. He'd hinted that he was up for promotion.

We would soon be entering the English Channel, passing between Dover and Calais in the Dover Straits.

Captain Armitage and Mrs Armitage were mingling among their passengers, many of whom they would see again on other cruises.

'So shall we be seeing you again, Miss Lacey?' he asked.

'I don't know. It has been a marvellous experience in many ways. The ship is beautiful and the service and food without fault. And I loved Norway to bits. I've never seen such spectacular scenery. But now I'm ready to go home, to my Latching, my sea, my pier and my beach.'

He laughed. 'Can we have that in writing? It's the perfect advertisement for cruising. A wonderful holiday and happy to go home.'

We didn't mention the negative side. Both Joanna and Oliver Carter were safely in custody and Geoff Berry had been removed from his duties. The older Suna had disappeared. It was doubtful if we would see her again. I felt sorry for her and wondered what hold Geoff Berry had manufactured over her. It might have been something as simple as an incorrect work permit.

'Latching is only an hour on the train from Southampton,' said Hamish Duncan, refilling my glass from the bottle he was carrying. 'Would I be offered a cup of coffee if I called by while the ship was on turnaround in dock?'

'Of course,' I said warmly. 'But I don't have a home yet. I have to do some serious house-hunting. But I should be happy to see you.'

'You still have my mobile number?'

'Yes.'

'Then we can keep in touch. I'm sorry you had such a rough time, but at least no one died on this cruise.'

'But they did,' said Max Russell, joining the group. 'We had one fatality. A Mr Edward Hale had a heart attack in his cabin and died. Very sad. An elderly gentleman travelling on his own.'

'But I knew him,' I said with a rush of emotion. 'I gave him my coach ticket for some excursion. He seemed very pleased to have it. A nice old gentleman.'

'You were probably the last person he spoke to. At least he enjoyed the trip, went with the majestic scenery of Norway on his mind.'

Mr Hale's death sobered me but at least it had not been a murder. Time had taken its normal toll.

Natasha joined us in one of her flamboyant outfits. This one was turquoise and orange stripes. She had recovered quickly from her ordeal, especially when she learned that she had lost nearly half a stone through the experience.

And she had an escort. Bill Quentin was at her side, cravat abandoned, looking casual in a blazer and an open-necked white shirt. They had plenty to talk about, lots in common and I'd seen them laughing together on deck.

'I'm going to make sure that you get a reward, dearie. You saved the company a half a million fraudulent claim. There's got to be a few thousand in it for you,' said Natasha, helping herself to a smoked salmon roll.

'Thank you. I'll be homeless in two weeks. I've got to find somewhere to live first.'

'Find somewhere with sea views. You love the sea so much. That's what you must have. There's only one condition.'

'What's that?'

'I want an invitation to your house-warming party,' she said.

I knew, without looking, that James was standing behind me. There was the essence of the man that enveloped my skin. It was a feeling that I never wanted to lose.

'I'll make sure you get one,' said James, answering for me.

I didn't mind James answering for me as his arm was round my waist. Quite possessively, I thought.